The Seventh Man

The Seventh Man

MY PART IN THE DEFECTION SCANDAL

by Geoffrey T. Alsop
as told to
Graeme Garden

EYRE METHUEN

First published in Great Britain 1981 by
Eyre Methuen Ltd
11 New Fetter Lane, London EC4P 4EE

Made and printed in Great Britain by
Richard Clay (The Chaucer Press) Ltd,
Bungay, Suffolk

British Library Cataloguing in Publication Data
Garden, Graeme
The seventh man.
I. Title
823'.914[F]   PR6057.A624/

ISBN 0-413-49080-7

Prologue

As I take up my pen* to record my involvement in what was to become the scandal not of one decade but of three, I feel that I must begin by setting certain matters straight. In studying the two defectors, the Third Man, and the rest, I have concentrated on looking for the human factor, trying in each case to reveal the man within. The confidential agent is not the trigger-happy adventurer of popular fiction; a gun for sale waiting in the basement room for the order which will release him, firearms blazing, to wreak havoc on a wicked foe. Nor is the field in which we operate the world of the desk and filing cabinet, the cup of tea, the inter-office memorandum; although to some extent it is. But it's a battlefield as well, though one on which the soldier cannot achieve the power and the glory.

Now and then, the secret war is brought out into the open. This scandal, which began with rumour at nightfall and went on to make our centres in London, Harlow and Brighton rock with its repercussions, is by no means a burnt-out case. Indeed, its powerful and continuing effect on all of England made me pursue my search to discover the heart of the matter. Discover it I did, and more beside, and as you will see, at the end of the affair, loser takes all.

Geoffrey T. Alsop
Stanley
October 1980

* I mean this metaphorically. This book is based upon typewritten transcripts of tape-recorded conversations between myself and Mr Garden, to whom I am indebted for his help in rearranging the narrative sequence and for advice on matters of style.

Unless otherwise stated in the text, all proper names have been changed to conceal the identities of the persons involved.

One

Wraiths of October mist were mustering in the hollows of the Heath like the shades of Department heroes long forgotten. Haloes of dirty ochre glowed around the streetlamps, which stood like rows of tarnished saints, their light reflecting from a road surface slick as a newly turned out slab of treacle toffee. A hint of wood-smoke in the air recalled the excited anticipation of a Guy Fawkes night before the fireworks begin.

The traffic through Hampstead moved slowly. I sat behind the wheel, scarcely glancing at the buildings that lined the street or the trees whose glistening leaves hung like dark scraps of leather. I had no interest in the once familiar scene. Hampstead now was so different from the charming village we had known when Helen and I had started out together in the two-room flat overlooking the Vale of Health. The village atmosphere had gone; now it had become more 'trendy' and commercial. 'Boutique Hill' Raymond Gray called it.

I steered through the jumble of traffic around the Whitestone pond, and the Austin Maxi purred reliably down the hill towards the A41, and Rickmansworth, and the man who was waiting there to meet me.

I swept up the Hendon Way towards the rendezvous, and the closer I got, the more the feeling of triumph began to fade. Perhaps it was disappointment at the nature of the truth I had uncovered, or perhaps it was the steadily growing wish to turn round and forget about the whole dismal business. Perhaps it was the weather. Certainly I was tired. That evening I had worked on at the office after the others had left, going over the files again and again, trying not to let enthusiasm over what I felt was the final breakthrough cloud my judgement. In the end I sat for a full hour at the desk, lit by a single 40-watt bulb – it was some months since the Office Ordnance department had clamped down on 60-watt bulbs for desk-lamp employment – staring at the files, my fingertips resting lightly on them, not reading them, touching them, hardly feeling them, and thinking. And I knew. Then I was sure I knew. And knowing, I knew where I must go and what I must do. With something strangely like regret I locked the files away in the office safe, turned out the light, locked up the office and went down in the lift, to let myself out into the damp October night and whatever it might hold. There was some confusion with the night security doorkeeper over my having a night key to the main door in my possession. He maintained – correctly – that night keys were only issued to staff of grade C clearance and above. I agreed and pointed out – also correctly – that as head of W Sector, MSI Section, I held temporary acting C grading and had done so for almost thirty years. He was a new man, unfamiliar with the intricacies of Section procedure, but despite protestations that it was more than his job was worth, he let me out to slip away into the night. As I passed through the door I asked, rather sharply, what he thought his job was worth, but his reply was lost in a sudden flurry of damp wind.

Now I was on the road, and it was late. As the Austin Maxi hissed over the gleaming tarmac towards Edgware, my digital watch – an early model you had to press a button on to illuminate the dial, thus requiring the use of both hands to tell the time – told me that it was fast approaching 20.40, but although I had barely had a full eight hours a night for almost a week, I was alert and ready.

Before leaving the office I had telephoned Helen to let

her know I would not be home for supper. She told me the carving fork had jammed the Colston and had broken half the sherry glasses, and asked what time I would be home for supper. I said I would not be home for supper, much to her dismay, but I cheered her up by suggesting she treat herself to one of the small Fray Bentos steak and kidney pies on the second shelf in the larder behind the pilchards.

Before setting off on my journey to Rickmansworth, I had consumed a hasty Doner Kebab and Baklava at the Pizza Workshop adjacent to the insignificant building in Stockwell which was Sector HQ. Now, as I drove on through the North London drizzle, I felt a dull knot of excitement like a leaden mass behind my waistcoat. Even the old warhorse Elsdon himself would not have denied himself that private thrill of impending satisfaction. He too would have probed and picked at it like a scab on his ankle, he too would have followed it through, he too would have sat in the frankly unsatisfactory light of a 40-watt bulb, touching the files until he knew. And he would have known. And when he had been sure he knew, he would have gone to Rickmansworth.

He would have gone to Rickmansworth as I did, for he had given me the route himself. By the A41 to Apex Corner Mill Hill, then left at the next roundabout on to the A410 through Stanmore, Harrow Weald, Hatch End, then on to the A404 north of Pinner, following the road for about three miles, then down the hill towards the town, and the canal.

It was on the approach to the traffic lights on Watford Way, beyond Hendon Central, that the car gave out. It felt as if a giant hand had reached out from the dark behind me to pull me back. I was travelling uphill, but nevertheless managed to coast the car into the side of the road. I struggled quickly but awkwardly across to the passenger door – banging my shin quite painfully on the gear lever – and got out, crouching behind the open door. I was fairly sure I had not been followed – Byfleet training dies hard – but if they had done something to the car, it was their bad luck that it had broken down on such a well-populated stretch of road. I took a deep breath. This was the first time I had thought of there being a 'they', or that 'they' might wish me harm. But now, so close to the end of the road, I could take no chances. I rubbed the mist and drizzle from my glasses with the paper tissue I kept up my sleeve, a habit dating from the days when I used to keep a linen handkerchief up my sleeve. The overcoat made me warm and damp and I was breathing heavily. Although I had done the training course at Byfleet, I had never worked in the field. Sixty was not a good age to start.

There was a call-box about a hundred yards behind me on my side of the road at the end of a parade of shops. After a quick look round to see there were no suspiciously parked cars, or seemingly casual loiterers, I broke from the car and scurried towards the telephone, bent double to keep a low profile. My only moment of possible exposure was as I hurried past the illuminated front of a fish and chip parlour, but business was slack and I thought I had got past unseen. Thankfully the phone in the call-box was operational, but the line to Transport Division was engaged. The night operator chatting to her boyfriend no doubt. I made a mental note to issue a memo. In the end I called the RAC, who promised instant attention. Now I needed somewhere to settle down for the long wait.

Bent double, I hurried back to the car. As I passed the fish and chip parlour, I caught a flicker of movement within, but reached the car unchallenged. It was not safe to stay with the car. Across the road, on the central island, was one of the clumps of pampas grass which the council always plant there. It took a full three minutes by my watch to check that I was not being observed; then, when there was a break in the traffic, I ran – still stooping – across the road and crouched among the tall pale stems, some broken, their feathered tops now bedraggled and bent down by the drizzle.

The passing traffic spattered me lightly with spray. A particularly heavy shower from the wheels of a passing articulated lorry had coated my spectacles with a muddy film, when dimly I saw the door of the fish and chip parlour swing open. A man came out and began to cross the road towards me. I could see that he held something in his right hand, hiding it inside the maroon nylon jacket he wore. There was nowhere to go. I froze.

The man trotted across the road and stopped in front of me. Crouching in the damp vegetation, a trickle of cold water edging down inside the collar of my heavy dark blue overcoat, I blinked up at him.

'I've been watching you,' he said. I swallowed. He grinned down at me. 'Caught short, was you?' he continued. 'Thought you might need this.' He took his right hand from the jacket and held out a roll of toilet paper.

'Thank you,' I said, tearing off two sheets, and cleaning my glasses.

Despite the kind offer of the friendly chippy – who was obviously clean – I decided to stay put. Apparently unmoved by my rejection of his proffered seat in the warm and a nice cuppa, he gave an awkward, understanding smile.

'I know, mate,' he said, stooping to punch me lightly on the shoulder, 'it's a real bugger, isn't it?' Then he left me, insisting that I keep the toilet roll.

As I huddled in the pampas grass, pulling up the damp and prickly collar of my overcoat around my neck, I reflected on the sequence of events that had brought me to this place. It had started thirty years before, in the days when Elsdon ran the Section. I can see his face now as he sat behind his desk – such a small desk for such a big man – and broke the news about the two traitors, Sturgess and McBain.* Although they had not been in MSI, the news

* By the time Elsdon did break the news to us, everyone in Section already knew about it from the newspapers, but most of us were gracious enough to feign surprise, although in my opinion Raymond Gray went

of their defection had come as a shock to us all. Later this was followed by the news that Jim Phibley had gone over to the other side. Not gone over suddenly, he had been turned by them years before. The great Jim Phibley, as great as Elsdon if you like. Greater in terms of personal expense rating, though not in security grading. And finally, devastatingly, a mole in of all places the royal household, and of all people the elegant patrician Sir Anthony Buntle. Buntle, the fourth man.

The wise men of the Department had nodded their heads, saying they had always known there would be a fourth man. Dobbs was the first to express the opinion that, if there was a fourth, then why not a fifth? And a sixth? Or a seventh? Or a hundred and seventh? Elsdon's curt memo had soon put an end to such wild speculation, but it was generally agreed, though seldom stated in the Department, that there must be a fifth man somewhere; but that was MI5's problem and nothing to do with us. Or so we thought.

The RAC man arrived and poured in the half gallon of petrol required to get me to the next service station. There I filled up the tank and continued my journey. The soggy toilet roll on the seat beside me, I pressed my foot almost to the floor and the Austin Maxi surged forward at an unfamiliar 45 mph over the long hill past the Northwood Hospital. Had I really so little idea then of the effect my discovery would have on Sector, on Section, on the Department, on the whole British Secret Service itself? Would I have hesitated if I had known? Would I have stopped the car, turned it round and made for home, following the A404 all the way to Wembley before cutting through to Acton and the welcoming glow of the simulated cokite gas fire in the lounge? Or would I have pressed on regardless of the turmoil I was to cause; the personal distress to Raymond

---

rather too far by saying 'Merciful God!' in a very loud voice and smiting his forehead with an open palm.

Gray, Dennis Dobbs, to Agnes, Clive Black and the others? Would I have spared 'S', current Head of Section – Elsdon long since retired, presumed dead – the bitter sense of betrayal? I believe that, if I had known at the time what was to happen, I would still have gone on, as I did, up the A404 seeking, not revenge, but a discharge of duty.

Duty, however, is a word with many meanings; according to the *Concise Oxford Dictionary* at least seven. But duty it was that drove me through that autumn night towards the fifth man, and a kind of Nemesis.

Water Goblin was moored, I knew, in the field belonging to Lodge Park Farm. Turning off the road, I eased the Austin Maxi down the bumpy farm track, switching off the headlights so as not to advertise my approach. In the darkness I drove into an old oil drum full of rubbish, which fell over with a clatter, but not a very loud one. I left the car there and walked across the field and along the canal bank, reading the names of the boats by the light of the pencil-torch I had signed out from Field Equipment that afternoon, just in case. In the daytime the field had been used by cows, and I picked my way carefully, trying to avoid the mooring pegs of the boats and other hazards, but without complete success.

The boat was not big, no more than twenty-five feet long, but bigger than the small cruiser – *The Bijou* – Helen and I had hired for a weekend on the river just after the war. We had spent the first afternoon gliding downstream with the current, in silence – at least I had said very little – and we had tied up the boat under a bank of willows which reached down to trail their leaves in the slow-moving waters. I had almost fallen in drawing a kettleful of water from the river to make tea. We had been sitting, dangling our bare feet in the cool river water, sipping our tea, when a dead cat had floated past.

A sudden gust of wind slapped the lapel of my overcoat

against my cheek, the sting of it bringing me back from that pool of memory. With a shudder I turned off the torch and stepped into the cockpit of *Water Goblin*. My right foot skidded on the wet deck surface, made greasy by the remains on my sole of what I had, seconds before, stepped in. No sound came from the boat, but bright light spilled out from the open hatch to the front bit of the craft. I stepped inside.

He was there, of course. By the gently whispering light of a butane lamp I saw him sprawled across the bunk. His legs were spread at awkward angles on each side of the small central table, one arm lay outstretched towards the bottle of Glenfarclas that stood balanced on the cushion, the other across his chest, his head resting to one side against the wall. The eyes were open. I reached forward to feel for a pulse in the neck.

'Hello,' he said. I found it impossible to speak. Where could this conversation begin? All my efforts, the searching, the thinking, the long drive up the A41, the A410 and A404 had left me weary, but I was there because I knew. I knew it all. He knew too. There would be no game of cat and mouse. If I could find the right words it would be man to man. Cards on the table. But where was the triumph? Was this to be no more than a sordid end to a sordid business? I had to make an opening, but even as I spoke the words, I felt their inadequacy:

'You are the fifth man.'

He rose from the bunk. I put out a hand to steady myself as *Water Goblin* tilted in the water at the shifting of his weight.

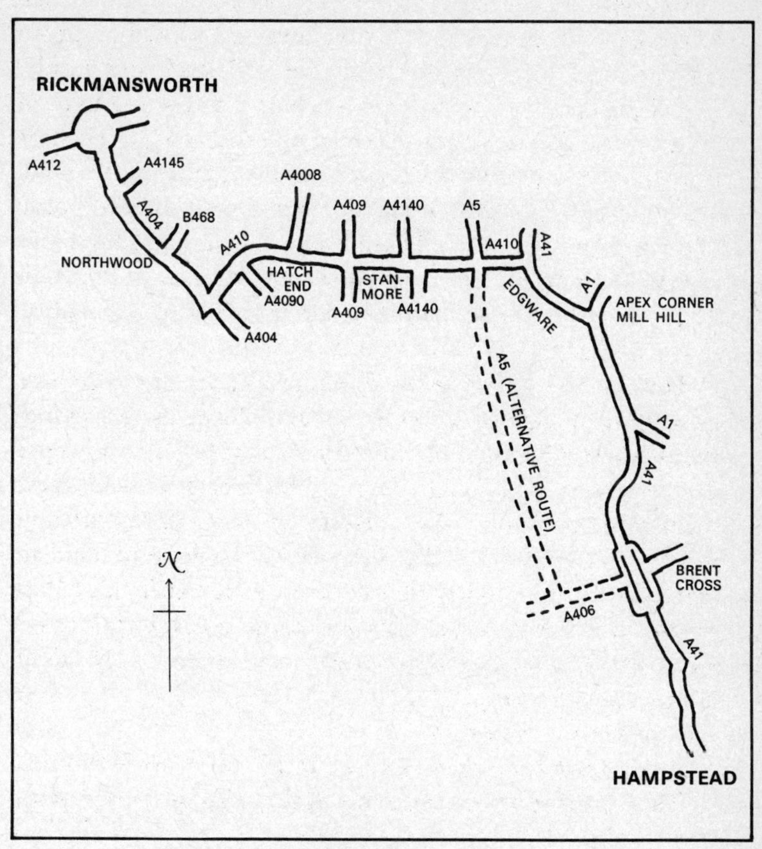

My route to Rickmansworth. (Not to scale.)

Two

When Section personnel get together over a cup of tea and a Garibaldi in their Staggered Refreshment Break,* and look back over the whole affair I dare say they will date the start of the long chain of events as 15 April, 1950. It was on that date that I was summoned to the office of S, Head of MSI Section, in the main building of our Stockwell headquarters.

At that time S was the only Section Head still known to his staff by code letter.† In fact the general practice of using code letters to identify Department and Section Heads had been abandoned shortly after the war. The incident which precipitated this change of policy was often retold to enliven an otherwise gloomy SRB. It appears that, in 1946, one of our Paris field-men took as his field-name – by the utmost coincidence – the real name of the Head of NEA Section, who was of course known to the agent only as Q. For several months, then, this field-man was operating under the name of Humphrey Bowen, under the misguided impression that the name was his own fiction and unaware that the real Bowen was a senior Department official. The matter only came to light when the genuine Bowen – Q – received a somewhat tart query from the accountants about his claim for entertainment expenses in Paris. Q, who had never been

* SRB.

† In keeping with the convention regarding proper names adopted throughout this book, S is not, of course, the Head of MSI Section's real coed letter.

to Paris in his life and indeed had no interest in the Paris operation, was naturally puzzled and later became rather annoyed when the accountants called for him to justify his claim for the costs of a large private party held at the Hotel George V, which costs included the hire of a cabaret featuring the services of a young lady and her performing donkey. Eventually the accountants traced the cause of the confusion and for a time things went rather stickily for the field-man.

After the Paris incident, the memo went out announcing that Department and Section Heads would henceforth be known to their subordinates by their real names, and that the booking of circus acts, however clever, would no longer be accepted as legitimate expenses by the accountants. Only Bill Elsdon stood up against the official line, and insisted that Head of MSI still be known only as S to his Section. Elsdon was known to be a great believer in tradition and capable of thunderous fits of anger when crossed, so his request was granted. That and many other traditions – important as they are to Section spirit – persist until today, which is why the names of Bill Elsdon and his successors as S are still held in high regard.

It was Bill Elsdon I was going to meet as I made my way that bright April morning from the Clitheroe Road annexe to the main building where he had his office. Although I had not been told the reason for the summons, I suspected that it may have had something to do with the recent discovery of a shortfall in the supply of Tipp-Ex typewriter correction fluid, for the ordering of which I had been temporarily partly responsible. With that in mind I had rehearsed my defence, which was that the current influx of untrained temporary typists had considerably increased the demand for correction fluid, and that my present position as acting under-assistant to Head of Stationery* did not, strictly speaking, include responsibility for the supply of such

* Head of Stationery at this date was S. J. Tombs. (S. J. Tombs is not of course his real name.)

materials as part of my working brief.

It is worth noting here that after completing the Byfleet training course, I had entered Section work and had risen quite rapidly to the post of Operational Assistant in M Section. After that, for some reason, I had spent almost two years seconded to Catering Section – on the administrative side, of course, working opposite Dennis Dobbs – and then Stationery. I did not care much for the way my career had been progressing, and when I entered his office to shake hands with S, I had decided on a bold approach and was determined to open my side of the dialogue by pointing out that the ordering of supplies is quite specifically the responsibility of permanent members of Stationery Division and not operational personnel on temporary loan from other parts of the Department. Imagine then my surprise and delight when S opened the interview by offering me a seat, a cup of tea and control of MSI Section's Sector W.

Naturally I accepted all three. S appeared pleased, and with the minimum of prompting from him, I agreed that, before relinquishing my present post, I would sort out the problem over supply and demand of Tipp-Ex.

So there I was, Head of Sector at the age of thirty-one. At this point it would be as well to point out the difference between Section and Sector in our branch of the Department.

The Department is MI6, which concerns itself exclusively with overseas intelligence* and is divided into twelve Sections. Each Section covers a specific geographical area, for example my own Section – MSI – is responsible for intelligence operations conducted in Medium-Sized Islands. These include Tasmania, the Falkland Islands, the Scillies, Canaries, and so on. Although MSI Section runs field-men in all these areas, it may well appear to the outside observer that our activities may be less dramatic than those of Sections

* As is well known, Sturgess and McBain operated within the Department. My own connection with their activities will be made clear in due course.

such as SA, LA, E, SR, or even M.* And so they are. But we have our moments. For a few heady hours in 1957 we were still running Cuba as one of our Medium-Sized Islands after the escalation of the revolution began, until our masters decreed that operational control should be handed over to LA, SR and M Sections together (with, I may add, some initial confusion of interests and effect). Indeed the immediate reaction of all three Sections was to saturate the island with field-men, many of whom were later caught up quite unprepared in the Bay of Pigs invasion – instigated by the then President of the United States (let us call him X) – and taken prisoner, much to the embarrassment of the Department, which followed standard procedure and disclaimed any responsibility for or knowledge of their presence and activities. Many of those field-men are still unaccounted for, although several managed to make their own way home, one of them by hi-jacking an internal flight and forcing the bewildered Cuban pilot at gunpoint to fly him to Miami. It has often been said that if the running of Cuba had been left in the hands of MSI Section, subsequent developments in the Gulf of Mexico would have been noticeably different.

However, we in MSI Section are not prone to bitterness or envy. When an island is taken from our sphere of interest and allocated to another Section because it has become – in Department jargon – a hot potato, we pride ourselves on feeling no sense of deprivation; rather we express an attitude of pride, as if a favourite child had passed the entrance examination to an acceptable boarding school. We regard it as a sort of graduation. We keep up a keen interest in our protégé and watch its progress with concern, and of course we are well aware that the only islands we 'lose' to other Sections are those which have become centres of hostile political activity, as has recently been the case in Malta and Gibraltar (both now lost to E and M Sections).

* SA: South African Section; LA: Latin American Section; E: European Section; SR: Soviet Russian Section; M: Miscellaneous Section.

With such widespread responsibilities, it became necessary in the late 1930s to divide MSI Section into two Sectors, E and W. E Sector is broadly speaking responsible for medium-sized islands in the Eastern Hemisphere and W Sector for those in the West. What Bill Elsdon was offering me that day in 1951 was operational control of parts of the Caribbean, Cuba (in those days still ours), the Falklands, the Azores, Newfoundland (strictly speaking a large island, but traditionally ours), and many others. You may imagine the terrific sense of responsibility I felt. When I told Helen the good news that evening she seemed pleased, although not at first quite able to take it in, her thoughts being largely on the guttering above the kitchen window, which I had failed to unblock over the weekend, pre-occupied as I was with the Tipp-Ex crisis.

Later, over a celebratory Cherry-B in front of the Aga, the full impact of my news struck her. Gutters were forgotten as the implications of my – albeit modest – rise in salary and position became clear to her. At once she set to making plans for future trips to what she was already thinking of as 'our' islands. It seemed a shame to dampen her newly-kindled enthusiasm for travel by reminding her that, as Head of Sector, I would very much be confined to the Stockwell headquarters. This check to Helen's dreams of lazy days among the islands brought a flutter to her lower lip and a quiver to the nylon ruffles on her bosom. Despite my memory of her hasty words on the subject of gutters earlier in the evening, I made a mental note to fetch home another two boxes of her favourite chocolate assortment next day. For the time being I managed to perk her up by pointing out that my new status – carrying with it not only a raise in salary but an increased allocation of leave – would allow us to extend our annual summer holiday in Skegness by at least three days. She wept at the news. That night, before retiring to bed, we warmly embraced.

Next morning I was at my desk as Head of W Sector, MSI Section, MI6. My first visitor was my opposite number, Head of E Sector, Raymond Gray. For many years Gray and I had been colleagues, and although his gaudy style was not always to my taste, we had, I think, developed a kind of mutual feeling of respect and trust. I was pleased to see a friendly face that morning, the burden of my new responsibilities heavy on my shoulders. I smiled a welcome as Gray's figure appeared in the doorway, clad in the familiar dark blazer and fawn slacks, the inevitable pink shirt, and – on this occasion – the lime green tie with mauve floral motif. Gray's ties were the talk and envy of many in the Department. My own opinion regarding ties is that a school, college, regiment or club tie will advertise as much of a man's character as he needs to. In our business, where observation is very much part of the game, you soon learn to tell a great deal about a man's personality by his choice of tie and the shine of his shoes. Gray invariably wore suede.

'Good morning, Gray,' I said, by way of a greeting.

'Wotcher cock!' he replied, and I was forced to smile at the incongruity of the rough cockney phrase spoken in Gray's cultured Eton and Cambridge tones – it was part of his charm. 'Welcome to the Legion of the Lost.'

'Thank you,' I said.

'This, I believe, calls for a celebratory tot,' he went on, but having unsuccessfully searched my new desk for the office bottle, Gray gave me a boyish grin and a playful punch on the shoulder, and left.

Business in the Medium-Sized Islands was sluggish that first month. Clearly this state of affairs was partly due to the fact that a considerable portion of our secretarial and switchboard allocation had been temporarily diverted to the European Sector. Something big, we were told, was up. I took advantage of this slack period by busying myself with organizing my desk and personal files, personally ensuring that the requisition form for two 60-watt bulbs was properly processed and taken seriously by Office Ordnance, and deciding where to hang the photograph of Stalin.* Since joining the Department, it had always been my practice to place a photograph of Stalin near my desk. I believe it sound policy to try and understand the thinking of the adversary, a theory shared by Field Marshal Montgomery, who kept a photograph of General Erwin Rommel in his caravan. His Rommel was my Stalin. For hours I would sit staring at the photograph of the bearded Russian, wondering what he was up to, what he was thinking, how he would react to the current situation, whatever it might be. Some thought it eccentric, and indeed it was a ploy which did not always work. At times, no amount of staring into those cold bespectacled eyes would help. I was never able to surmise, for example, how Stalin would have handled the Tipp-Ex crisis.

For the next year I immersed myself in the hurly-burly of Sector life. Raymond Gray had been my first visitor, and thirteen months later he was to be my second. He came in, clutching a bottle of Bell's in one hand, a copy of that morning's *Daily Express* in the other.

'What about these comedians, eh?' he chuckled, waving the newspaper in my face.

'Comedians?' I inquired, not having had time that morning to scan the *Telegraph*, a heavy shower in the night having once again rendered the gutter situation at home acute. As a result, I had been obliged to spend the breakfast hour perched on top of the coke bunker, elbow deep in wet leaves.

'You have read about it, haven't you?' said Gray, helping himself to my newly delivered cup of tea and generously reinforcing it with a slug from his bottle.

'Well,' I replied, playing for time, 'I glanced at it, I did glance at it. Briefly. Missed out on a few details, you know. Just had a glance really. Gutters . . .'

* Stalin was the cover-name of the Russian leader Joseph Vissarionovich Dzhugashvili.

Gray smiled and gulped a mouthful of tea and Scotch as I turned to the entertainments page, vainly scrutinizing the columns for some good, bad or even scandalous news of Jewell and Warriss, the Two Pirates, Norman Evans or the Crazy Gang. At the time Jewell and Warriss were my particular favourites on the wireless – I had never seen them on stage, where I am told they were most entertaining – although I had been very amused watching the Two Pirates on George Attercliffe's new television set. It was my opinion that they were suspended on wires for the act, but George's wife Muriel disagreed, as did Helen. Today, almost thirty years later, I stick to my guns.

'What comedians?' I asked at length.

'Front page, old son, front page,' said Gray, further augmenting and consuming my tea.

Turning to the front page I was horrified to see the coverage and photographs of two of our men who had defected to the other side. To Raymond Gray, these men were 'the comedians'. To me, even then, they were something else.

Gray's description of the defectors as the comedians became accepted terminology in the Department, and eventually in the Secret Service as a whole. As a matter of fact, Gray went on to invent several slang names for the various parts of our organization. He it was who designated the senior female assistants in Agnes Muir's Records Division as Aunties, our cover-up specialists as Whitewashers, multiple agents as Maggots, and long-term undercover agents as Moles. In time these names caught on and by the mid-fifties Raymond Gray had become the Department's unofficial Head of Jargon. In 1952 our masters instituted a three-monthly meeting of all Sector Heads for a jargon conference presided over by Gray. At these meetings, he would put forward any new slang names which had come to him, and as they were generally considered witty, they would be approved, and memos sent out admitting them into the argot of the Department. I maintained that the time devoted to these jargon conferences could have been better spent, but what protests I made were ignored. It was thought that my objections arose from resentment of the fact that my own Sector had been christened at an early date the Winkle-pickers.

The comedians, of course, were Sturgess and McBain. But as I stared at their photographs on the front page of the *Daily Express*, 26 May, 1951, my mind was not concerned with Gray's amusing nomenclature, nor with his appropriation of my tea. I recognized their faces. I knew those men.

I had met them.

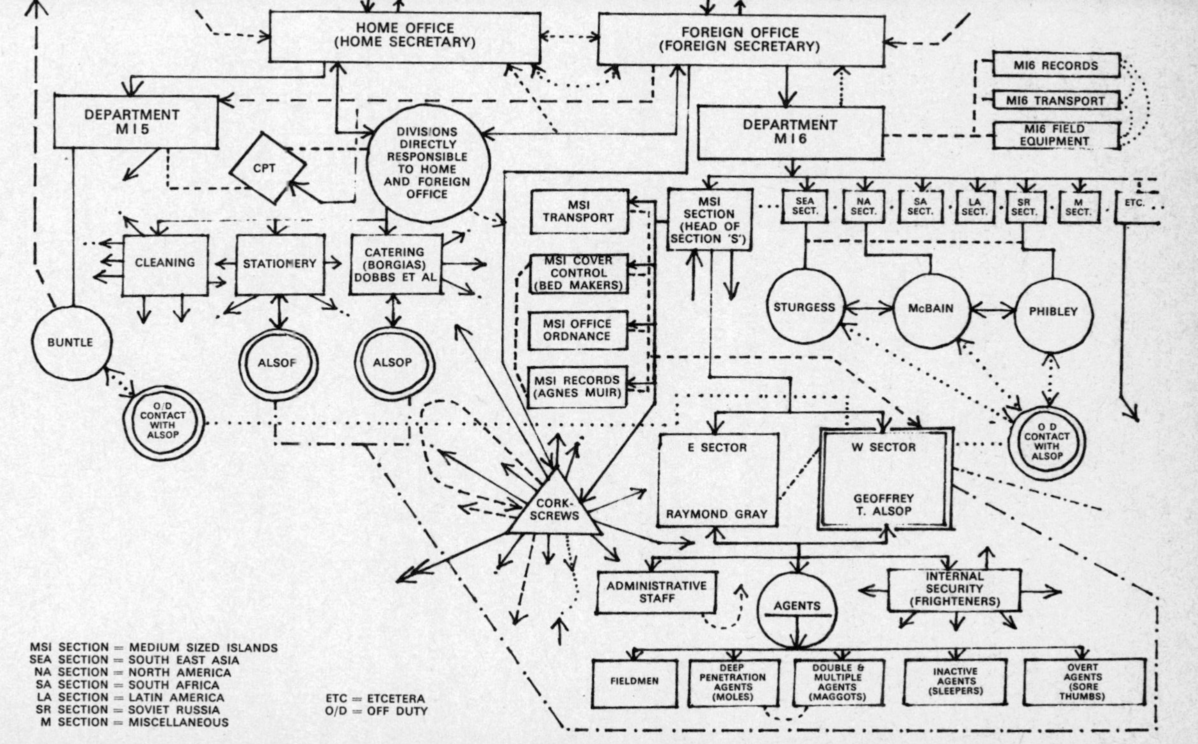

Diagram to clarify the inter-relationships between Departments, Sections and Sectors, and to indicate Geoffrey T. Alsop's place in the system.

Three

My first and only contact with Gus Sturgess came early in 1951, in the Gents' toilet at Stockwell Headquarters. I had been Head of W Sector for less than a year, still very much a new boy and finding my feet. Our brief encounter came at the end of a difficult session with Agnes Muir, queen of the Records Division. Agnes was something of a legend in the Department. Even Section Heads had been known to cringe before one of her famous onslaughts. She ruled her staff – the Aunties, as they came to be known in the Sixties – with what Raymond Gray described as 'an iron fist in a titanium glove'. As a matter of fact, although we certainly had our differences from time to time, Agnes and I developed a sort of rapport during my years as Head of W Sector until her retirement at the age of 75 in the early nineteen-sixties. We were never actually close – with Agnes that would have been impossible – but we came to recognize in each other certain similarities in outlook. An example of this occurred during one of the increasingly frivolous jargon meetings in 1958. Raymond Gray had just pushed through his recommendation that henceforth the De-Briefers be known as the Knicker-Snatchers,* and had gone on to propose that Upper Classification Field Memos be printed on cheese-and-onion-flavoured paper, for the benefit of the agents who might be obliged to swallow them. I noticed at the time that Agnes

* In 1960 an official Jargon Update was issued by MI6 administration changing this title to Vampires, in my opinion an improvement.

and I were the only ones present who did not appear to find these proposals amusing. Our eyes met across the table. That is as close as I, or anybody else, ever came to intimacy with Agnes.

We were never, however, friends. Agnes had no friends. She was one of the tough nuts in the Department and cherished her reputation. Over sixty years old in 1951, she was to go on dominating Records with a fierce independence for many years. Long after the introduction of Computer Data Storage, Agnes insisted that facts alone were never enough, so every request for information had to pass through her hands, so that she could return, not mere data, but the personal recollections, cross references, hunches and what she called her 'frissons' that could reveal so much more to the inquirer than the plain facts requested. She was well served by her team of Aunties – a somewhat misleading name, many of them being reasonably young and even considered attractive, and not all of them women – some of whom could locate one of Agnes' hand-written dossiers, complete with their marginal observations – what Agnes called 'the meat on the bone' – from the appropriate heap within a week or two of the request being received.

In appearance, Agnes was said to provoke a mixture of pity and horror, although that is perhaps to overstate the case. Clive Black – who rarely spoke at all, but when he did it was with considered and considerable effect – surprised us all one day by observing in the canteen that Agnes reminded him of 'a raddled old man in drag wearing a costume apparently constructed of moss and topped with an amateur bird's nest of wire wool'. None of us knew what to say. Coming from Black this speech was unusually long – there were those who suggested that he had spent several weeks making it up – but while cruel, his description was fundamentally accurate. Agnes' hairstyle was at best haphazard, and she habitually dressed in old and crumbling knitwear of a dun green colour. Invariably a smouldering Woodbine hung from her lower lip, and she was rarely without a tumbler of Scotch on her desk, a brand known as Laphroaig. I once accused her, by way of a joke, of drinking French whisky – 'la' being the French feminine definite article, and 'phroaig' being a pun on 'frog'. Although Dilys, a pretty little Auntie, found my witticism cause for a giggle, Agnes was unimpressed. Agnes was a character. She was the butt of a great deal of good-natured banter, but I take it as a sign of good taste among her critics that nobody ever made reference to her moustache.

It was at the beginning of May, 1951, that I had my first contretemps with Agnes. It had been two weeks since I had asked her Records Division to furnish me with details of the paper-clip allocation to my Sector; there never seemed to be enough of them, and those we had were of frankly inferior quality, the result being that several memos and sets of documents were being muddled. On one occasion the third page of a confidential report on the suggested colour scheme for the third floor corridor became mixed up with some announcements concerning the Secretaries' Rest Room teaspoon and a disciplinary memo on the subject of whistling in the lift, and actually ended up pinned to the Sector Bulletin Board for all to see. This was not a state of affairs I was prepared to tolerate.

I had been Head of W Sector for barely a year, so rather than tackling Agnes herself, I had submitted my request to her First Assistant, Elsie Cadwallader. Elsie was the exact opposite of Agnes, small and frail with large spectacles which gave her the look of a startled bushbaby – an animal made familiar, to those who owned a television set, by George Cansdale, a great favourite of Helen's – and given to dressing in pastel shades, particularly pink. Shortly after her arrival at Stockwell, she had been dubbed by the Department wags as 'Precious Little Else'. Where Agnes was foul-mouthed, Elsie was prim; where Agnes was seldom sober, Elsie was never seen to drink; where Agnes roared, Elsie wept; Agnes the dragon, Elsie the mouse. They shared a basement flat in Clapham.

I had discovered that the monthly allocation of paper-clips to Sector was by weight. All I was asking from Records was a simple formula – how many paper-clips by number were we getting in our monthly two ounces? Armed with this information I would have been able to draft a sensible memo to Dawking of Stationery. A simple enough request, yet I had been made to wait two full weeks for a response. Perhaps I spoke too severely to Elsie when I returned to Records demanding an explanation. Her face quivered, her shoulders shook and she burst into tears, a cascade of hair-pins pattering on to the papers on her desk. As I tried, with no success, to comfort her, I heard Agnes bellowing down the corridor.

'Rapist!' she screamed as she blundered into the room.

'Not so,' I replied in an attempt to pacify her.

'Men!' she snarled, whisky slopping from the tumbler in her hand. My attention distracted by the amber droplets spattering on to the dusty lino, I didn't notice her knee driving towards me. It was a glancing blow, but disturbing. Luckily she was unable to follow through, as she lost her balance and fell down in a sort of squatting position. Her grey hair had always seemed to have a life of its own, but as she made sharp contact with the floor I swear I saw it tilt.

'Please, Agnes,' I gasped, 'it's about paper-clips.'

'Balls!' she roared as I edged behind a chair before she could focus on me again. 'You're trying to get your leg over my assistant.'

Nothing could have been further from my mind, and I said so, which brought a renewed burst of wailing from Elsie.

'You're all the same,' growled Agnes, struggling to her knees with a dangerous look in her good eye, 'you're all only after one thing.'

'I'm not surprised,' I said. 'Efficient office management relies on an adequate supply of paper-clips.'

'Bloody paper-clips?' she yelled. 'You're not bothering her with bloody paper-clips?'

'It has been two weeks,' I pointed out, judging my distance from the door.

'Can't you see she's in a state?' said Agnes, dragging herself to her feet with a fearsome crackling in her knees. As far as I could see, Elsie was permanently in a state, but now was not the time to mention it. Agnes swallowed a generous mouthful from the tumbler, and smacked her lips, causing her teeth to rattle ominously, and put a protective arm around Elsie's shoulder. 'Don't you know there's a flap on,' she asked me. 'Don't you realize this girl has more on her plate than bloody paper-clips?' She cradled the head of her weeping assistant, driving the bridge of Elsie's spectacles hard against her nose, causing the little woman to whimper.

'What flap?' I asked, reaching stealthily for the door handle.

'Tibet, you pratt-faced fanny!' explained Agnes.

'Tibet?' I riposted. 'That's miles away.'

'Judas Priest! It's like talking to a child,' exclaimed Agnes, quite unfairly. 'Look, the word is out that the Chinks are cooking up an invasion of Tibet. Probably this very year. That young pipsqueak Gosset from M Section has been pestering Elsie for the last month to dig up any information she can find on what military, economic or political use Tibet could possibly be to any other nation in the world. He's been at her every day.'

'You really think the Chinese will take Tibet?' I asked, inching the door open behind me.

'Of course they won't,' she replied. 'Young Gosset is only hanging around because he's after her body. Just like the rest of you. Any excuse. With Gosset it's Tibet. With you, God save us, it's paper-clips.'

By now I had the door half open, which gave me the courage to request an answer to my query by the next morning.

'Why don't you just piss off and leave us alone?' inquired Agnes, hugging Elsie's head so tightly that one of the assistant's large imitation pearl clip-on ear-rings plopped off her lobe and trundled under the radiator. Taking advantage of this diversion, I dodged out of the office and shut the door behind me.

I had made my point, and handled a tricky situation rather well, I thought. Even so, the encounter had left me feeling drained, and furthermore had taken up a considerable portion of the lunch-break, which meant that now I would only have time to gobble the spam and piccalilli sandwich that Helen had prepared for me that morning, washed down with a spoonful of Camp coffee essence stirred into the thermos flask of warm water I had brought in with me. That day, I thought, the *Daily Telegraph* crossword would remain unsolved.

Call it devilment if you will, but I decided at two o'clock – officially the end of lunch – that I would tackle the crossword willy-nilly. Accordingly I made my way to the Gents' toilet in the basement, planning to seclude myself in a cubicle for ten minutes or so to grapple with a few clues.

On entering the Gents', I was disturbed to find another man already there, combing his hair in the mirror above the washbasin. I was about to slip into a cubicle behind him, when I caught his eye in the mirror. He was smiling at me. Not wishing to be seen entering the cubicle with the *Telegraph* folded to display the crossword, thus revealing my intentions, I decided on subterfuge. I changed direction and made my way to the urinals, unbuttoned and stood facing the porcelain, meaning to wait there until the other fellow had gone before sneaking into the closet and locking the door. It was with surprise and some concern that I saw the man, who had finished with his hair, saunter across and stand next to me, open his flies, turn towards me, and smile again. I avoided his eye.

Of course I was not able to perform. What struck me as odd was that neither was he. We stood together in silence. Not a drop. I felt as if the *Daily Telegraph* was burning into my armpit. The man stood beside me and out of the corner of my eye I could see that his face was turned towards me, still smiling.

Mercifully, after what seemed like minutes, the urinal flushed. At the sound of gushing water I feigned relief and muttered, 'Ah, that's better. I needed that.' My companion chuckled in a knowing sort of way. Still I dared not look him in the face. As the water gushed down and swirled away into the drain, I noticed him taking something out of his pocket with his free hand and popping it into his mouth. I soon knew what it was. A clove of garlic. Neither of us made a move until long after the cistern had ceased, then suddenly the man leaned over and peered into my stall. He looked down and smiled, then enveloped me in a cloud of garlic fumes as he spoke.

'Ah well,' he said, 'we can't have everything.'

As I turned away to fasten my flies, he patted me on the behind. All thoughts of tackling the crossword now abandoned, I dropped my copy of the *Telegraph* on top of the crumpled paper towels in the wire bin beside the washbasins and left the toilet. I am not, of course, a fool or a prude. It is common knowledge that several members of the Department are practising homosexuals. In 1951 their deviation was regarded as a crime, but I have always been broad-minded enough to believe that those born with this unfortunate affliction should be allowed to live their own lives with whatever happiness and dignity they are able to achieve, as long as they keep themselves to themselves. Helen agrees with me, although she naturally prefers not to discuss the matter. However, even after many years in an organization which seemed, at times, actively to encourage abnormal behaviour, I can still get flustered by an overt approach in a public place. Nowadays, of course, it happens very rarely.

Leaving the Gents', I made my way up to my third-floor office by the stairs. The lift was slow and likely to be crowded, and I had no wish to bump into any colleagues out of my office a good ten minutes after the lunch-break had finished. As I reached the first-floor landing opposite Bill Elsdon's office I saw his door begin to open. I hesitated on the top step, wondering whether to hurry down to the half-landing until Elsdon had gone, or whether to try and make it round the corner and up the stairs before he saw me. I was still hesitating when a man emerged from the office, and I noted with relief that it was not Bill Elsdon. He was a stocky man of average height, with brownish hair and a kindly, lived-in sort of face. As he turned, he saw me, and he smiled. Not feeling up to a second confrontation so soon after the first, I did not smile back.

'Hello,' he said.

'Yes,' I replied.

'You're Alsop, aren't you? Bill Elsdon's been telling me all about you.'

'Oh,' I said, flattered, 'I hope you didn't believe all of it.'

'Oh, I believed all of it,' he said.

'Oh, well,' I said, by way of making conversation.

'I believe you've taken over W Sector. From what I hear, you're running a pretty tight ship. Good work.'

He held out his hand to be shaken. As I hesitated, he smiled.

'My name's Phibley,' he said, 'Jim Phibley.'

I was impressed. I shook his hand warmly, delighted to be the recipient of his praise. So this was the famous Jim Phibley, joining MI6 from Special Operations Executive in 1940, worked in Iberian Section in 1941, by 1942 in charge of North Africa and Italy, then in 1944 promoted to be Head of the newly formed Russian Section. Later to serve in the field as Head of Turkish Operations, then First Secretary to the British Embassy in Washington, Phibley was the golden boy of his generation in the Department, tipped by many to be a future Head of MI6. None of us had any idea at the time, of course, that Phibley had been working for the Russians since 1934.

I thanked him profusely for his kind words. Suddenly I noticed that his smile had faded, and that he was looking past me over my left shoulder. Turning round, I saw the man who had spoken to me in the Gents' carefully studying the clubs and societies notice board by the side of the lift. I recalled hearing the lift doors open as Phibley had emerged from Elsdon's office. The man by the notice board would have been able to overhear our conversation. I turned back to Phibley, who released my hand, nodded and said:

'Well then.'

'Well,' I rejoined, 'I'll try to keep up the good work.'

'Well, good,' he replied.

The man by the notice board coughed or murmured, it was hard to say which. Phibley turned away and hurried down the stairs. I watched him go. Before going round the corner to the half-landing, he paused and looked back up at me.

'Flies,' he whispered, and was gone.

I hastily buttoned myself up. By now it was sixteen minutes past two and high time that I was at my desk. I was startled by a loud knocking behind me, and turned to see the man from the Gents' rapping at Elsdon's door.

'Come!' roared Elsdon from within.

The man looked round at me and winked. Ignoring him, I made my way to the foot of the stairs, but as I passed him he reached out to grasp my arm. I stopped and looked him full in the face. I was in no mood for further monkey business. To my surprise, he was no longer smiling, and his expression could only be described as earnest.

'Keep an eye on Dobbs,' he said, then with a loud 'Hello!' he flung open the door and sprang into Elsdon's office.

As I made my way up to the third floor I puzzled over his warning. Dennis Dobbs had been my immediate superior in Catering during my attachment to that Division. For what reason should I be advised to keep an eye on him? Admittedly his lamburgers had not been well received, but basically we all knew him to be a sound man. To be perfectly honest, I resented the cheek of this apparent stranger in criticizing our catering arrangements, knowing as I did – and from the inside – the efforts made by that Division to provide a nourishing and balanced diet for Department staff. Although I and many others preferred to bring a packed lunch to Stockwell headquarters for reasons of economy, I would defend to the death the palatability of Catering's attempts.

What I did not know at the time, nor was I to know until Raymond Gray showed me the newspaper photograph of the comedians, was that the man I had encountered in the Gents' was none other than Gus Sturgess.*

* This chance meeting between Sturgess and Phibley, only a few weeks before the defection by Sturgess and McBain, has never been reported elsewhere. I am sure, however, that my recollection is accurate. Sturgess had recently been sent home from Washington in disgrace. Phibley, who was serving in the British Embassy in Washington at the time, had aroused the suspicions of the CIA, who had alerted MI6. It would be logical to assume that both had been called in to the Department for interrogation. However, my later discoveries were to indicate a very different interpretation of the event.

Four

To the best of my knowledge I never actually spoke to Donald McBain. I saw him once at the Records Division Christmas party at the end of 1950. As I stepped over him, Agnes told me that he was Donald McBain, or rather she told me she thought he was Donald McBain, Agnes never having been good with names. It was rather a rowdy evening, as I recall – Agnes had supervised the mixing of the fruit cup herself – and I left early when the horseplay started to get out of hand. As you will by now have realized, I am in no sense a fuddy-duddy, but I felt that it was time to withdraw when Dennis Gosset of M Section started being very irresponsible with a banana. It is worth noting, in passing, that McBain at this time was Head of the Foreign Office American Section.

I arrived home that evening well after nine o'clock. Helen was dozing on the lounge sofa by the electric fire, so I did not disturb her as I slipped into the kitchen to brew up the Bournvita and tackle the washing up. For security reasons, wives and girlfriends were not invited to within-Department functions – just as it was forbidden for personnel to take work home from the office – so our private and professional lives were kept very much apart. Helen has never really known what I actually do. This is not a state of affairs she has ever been happy with, which is why, before leaving for work on the morning of the party, I had presented her with a bottle of Bristol Cream to keep her company until I should return.

While the hot water was running into the sink, I crept

into the hall to check the cupboard under the stairs where we kept the hoover and the brooms and dusters. Nobody opened that cupboard when I was not in the house, but the small slip of paper I had wedged between the top of the door and the lintel had been dislodged. The door had been opened. Helen had found her Christmas present.

On Christmas morning, a few days later, Helen feigned great delight when she unwrapped the gift, which pleased me. It was to give us many weeks of useful service, until the occurrence of what we called the 'Minor Disaster'. I had been cooking some thick pea soup in it, when the valve at the top must have become blocked, and the pressure inside blew out the plug. A boiling green fountain hit the ceiling and the steaming mixture sprayed about the room. The shriek of the escaping vapour was appalling. Luckily, Helen was not in the kitchen at the time, but my waistcoat and trousers were spotted with stains before I could duck under the table. Helen was horrified when she saw the damage done to the kitchen of which she was so proud – I had finished redecorating it in peach and magnolia only three weeks before – and no amount of Bristol Cream would calm her. At last I was able to persuade her that the damage was only superficial, and she went to bed reassured, after I had promised to clean the soup off the paintwork that night, and that next day she would find a spotlessly clean kitchen when she came downstairs to lunch.

The clean-up took longer than I had anticipated and it was past midnight by the time I had swabbed the walls and ceiling, and sponged my trousers and waistcoat, leaving them to dry on the clothes-rack over the Aga. The result next morning was that I overslept. In spite of skipping breakfast and running to the station – this being long before I was allocated my own motor car – I arrived at Stockwell at four minutes past nine. Knowing that the lift would be too slow, I hurried up the stairs. On the first landing I ran straight into Bill Elsdon. He was looking impatient, restless. I hoped that my past time-keeping record would go in my favour, but I felt obliged to make some explanation.

'Pressure cooker. Blown,' I gasped.

'Blown?' asked Elsdon, suddenly concerned.

'Yes. Pressure cooker,' I replied.

'What does that mean?'

'Well, it's a sort of pan you can cook things in quickly. You clamp down –'

'Oh, you mean a real pressure cooker? That's all right.'

'Made an awful mess,' I explained.

Elsdon put his arm round my shoulder and led me over to the clubs and societies notice board by the lift.

'Conversational tone,' he said, 'okay?'

'Yes,' I said.

'We have a commercial traveller,' he murmured, 'a bird of passage. A need to go.'

'I see,' I said, not yet understanding.

'That's right,' he smiled, pointing at the latest snooker club draw. 'Rather urgent. Our chum has to be away tomorrow.'

Two Aunties hurried past, giggling at some piece of gossip, their heels clipping loudly on the linoleum. Elsdon and I studied the snooker draw. By now I had realized that he had something of importance to impart, and that he wished whatever it was not to be overheard by anybody else. Before we spoke again, we waited until the Aunties had disappeared, each into his respective office.

'I hate to drag you away from your desk,' went on Elsdon, looking for all the world like a man discussing Raymond Gray's chances in his first frame against 'Tiger' Morris of SEA Section, 'but I need a little leg-work and you're the only man I can trust.'

What had started as a bad day was turning into something important.

'Fine,' I said, smiling and nodding.

'Petty France,' he said quietly.

'Passport job?' I asked, in a normal tone of voice, stil nodding, as men do when discussing mundane matters of the day.

'Passport in the name of Smith,' said Elsdon, 'and for God's sake stop nodding your head.'

Sometimes I felt Elsdon lacked subtlety in his appreciation of undercover operations. A tendency to underestimate those little outward physical signals that would help an agent blend naturally into his surroundings.

'You want me to pick up a passport from Petty France for a man called Smith,' I said, shaking my head.

Elsdon sighed. 'Yes,' he whispered.

I laughed loudly. Elsdon, I am sorry to say, looked startled, unable to appreciate the extra touches I was adding to our performance.

'Look,' he said, rather more loudly than I considered prudent, 'when you get there ask for a man called Heinkel. No one else, do you understand? Heinkel will give you the passport.'

I laughed again – one never knew who might be observing us – and clapped him on the back. 'Yes,' I chuckled, 'yes, yes, very good.'

Elsdon took hold of my overcoat lapel and swung me round to face him. The door of his office opened and Christine, his secretary, called out to him. 'Mr Elsdon, you call from America,' she announced.

'Tiger Morris doesn't stand a chance,' I exclaimed in a voice loud enough for her to hear. Then I laughed again, this time derisively.

'Hold the call for a moment, Christine,' said Elsdon tersely. When she had gone back into the office, he took a deep breath through his nose and turned to face the notice board. He had got the hang of it now and was giving an excellent impression of a man losing his temper in some sporting dispute. 'Alsop,' he began, quietly and evenly but with great earnestness, stabbing a finger at the snooker notice, 'our traveller must go tomorrow. That means he must have the passport tonight. Do you have a safe drop?'

'Yes,' I whispered.

'Good,' said Elsdon, and sighed.

As it happened, I had several safe drops, but only one would be operational at any given time. Every few weeks I would check out a new drop, although I had never as yet had cause to use one. Only three or four days before this conversation I had checked my currently operational drop, which happened to be situated conveniently near my home.

'Where is it?' whispered Elsdon, impersonating a man having difficulty controlling his impatience.

'Acton,' I murmured in an offhand sort of way, then exclaimed in a loud voice: 'What? Barker, win the Snooker Rose Bowl? You must be off your chump,' and then, switching with practised ease into a confidential mutter, 'you know my address. About a hundred yards down the road running parallel to the back of the terrace. Clump of trees and scrub. Sizeable area. Dead ground. One tree, not very big, has a rotten trunk. Hole at top of trunk, big enough to hold delivery. Safe drop. Checked out a couple of days ago. Can't miss it. Happens to have white cross painted on trunk.'

'Speak up,' said Elsdon, putting on a cross voice. I repeated the instructions and he nodded. 'By eleven,' he said.

'Tonight? Will do,' I replied.

'Thank God,' said Elsdon, and went into his office. I stayed studying the notice board for a few minutes to consolidate my cover, then made my way past Elsdon's door towards the stairs. The door was ajar as I passed it and I could hear Elsdon exploding into the telephone: 'Yes, I told you, we got your cable yesterday. It's under control. I've fixed it. How many times do I have to tell you not to phone me at the office?'

After his performance at the notice board, I was often to

wonder, as I did when I heard him on the telephone, whether or not he was putting on an act.

As we finished our macaroni cheese supper that evening, I announced to Helen that I was going out for a while.

'What for?' she asked.

'For a walk.'

'You?'

'Yes,' I replied, a little tetchily, for it had been a trying day.

At the passport office they had denied all knowledge of a Mr Heinkel. Having waited in the queue for almost half an hour, and then fifteen minutes more while they searched for Mr Heinkel, I was prepared to accept second best when a pimply youth returned to tell me the nearest thing they had was a Mr Hinckley. He would do, I said, and was shown into a bare waiting-room with a bench and a single-bar electric fire with no plug on its flex.

I waited in the room for the best part of an hour. During this time two people looked in at me and then disappeared before I could ask them about Hinckley or Heinkel. Eventually a fat young man entered and closed the door behind him.

'Hinckley?' I asked.

He made no reply, but sifted through some forms. At length he spoke.

'Stand up and take off your clothes,' he said.

I did neither and he became rather excited, until another fat young man burst in and demanded, 'Are you Alsop?'

The first fat young man said no, his name was Pratt. I rose and announced myself. The second fat young man apologized for the first fat young man who had been recently transferred from Immigration and hadn't got the rules right yet.

After Pratt had been persuaded to leave, the second fat young man produced a passport from his pocket. I took it from him and scanned it briefly. It was made out in the name of Smith with a blurred photograph that could have been almost anyone. I slipped it into my breast pocket.

'Thank you,' I said. 'Heinkel?'

'Armitage,' said the second fat young man, and left with a wink.

On leaving the house that evening after supper, I made my way to the Crossed Keys. I went there, not for a fortifying drink, but to borrow the dog. A dog is always useful cover for movement at night, and the landlord was grateful for an offer to exercise the beast. By ten o'clock I was on my way to the safe drop with Pongo the Irish Setter straining at his lead.

No street lighting illuminated the scrubby copse which was my destination. Pongo pulled me from side to side through the darkness, intent on following trails of scent known only to himself. He was a strong animal and I had difficulty in finding my memorized route to the safe drop tree. It had rained during the evening and the moist earth threw up who knows what smells to intrigue the dog. I have never been fond of animals and it is with understandable annoyance that I concluded that Pongo had dragged me off course when I reached what should have been the site of the rotten trunk to find nothing but churned up turf. Pongo was frisky, but I dared not let him off the leash. In his present mood he would have disappeared in a trice, and I had more important work to do than chasing a runaway Setter.

I tied the dog's lead to the base of a gorse bush. Mercifully Pongo did not bark, but licked my face a good deal. Striking a match, I tried to find my bearings, and I was horrified to discover that I was in the right place, but the tree had gone. Widening the circle of my search I discovered a pile of newly cut logs, and I was forced to the conclusion that my safe drop had been, within the last two days, cut down. Now I understood the significance of the white cross painted on its trunk.

I had, as Raymond Gray would have put it, trouble. Elsdon had told me that our man had to be out by tomorrow. At eleven o'clock the bird of passage would be looking for his passport in a safe drop that no longer existed. Clearly it would be a breach of basic security for me to wait at the site to hand it over to him in person. There was only one thing to do.

Cursing myself for the lack of foresight in not bringing a torch – a mistake I was never to make again – I lit another match and approached the nearest pile of logs. Kicking and shoving them aside, I was at last relieved to discover the tree trunk I needed. It was now cut into a section about six feet long, with the hollow part at one end, the white cross still clear. Being narrow, the tree was quite easy to manoeuvre. I dragged the trunk out of the pile towards its previous location. The ground there was wet and muddy, which was all to the good. Laying down the length of tree, I began to kick and heel a hole in the earth. By ten forty-two I judged the hole to be deep enough. I dragged the tree-trunk over to the depression, stood it up and began to kick the earth around it. My shoes were caked with mud and I flinched at the thought of what Helen would say if she were to catch me cleaning them in the morning.

In my line of country it is always necessary to maintain a sense of proportion. My worries about Helen's reaction to the state of my shoes were nothing compared to the importance of the task in hand. At eleven pm our agent, Smith, would arrive expecting to pick up his passport from a hollow tree with a white cross on it. By five minutes to eleven, the tree was where he expected to find it, unstable but erect. Panting with the unaccustomed exercise, I stamped down the last of the loose earth, then reached into my hip pocket, pulled out the passport and slipped it into the hollow at the top of the resurrected trunk. My part of the mission was complete. As soon as I had returned Pongo to the Crossed Keys, I could make my way home, and whatever Helen might say, that night my bed-time Bournvita would contain a generous measure of gin.

I moved away to where I had left the dog. I bent down to release the lead. As I did so, a shadowy figure rose suddenly from the gorse bushes and leapt, roaring, through the darkness towards me.

Five

The Whittington Hospital is a grim and forbidding building in Highgate. It was in one of its gloomy wards that I found myself the next day. Dennis Dobbs had been rushed there after his cycling accident, and I had popped in to see him at lunchtime after I had filed my report on the previous night's events to Bill Elsdon's office.

As I made my way down the dim, ether-smelling labyrinth of corridors towards his bedside, I was nagged by a persistent thought. Why had the man in the Gents' urged me to keep an eye on Dobbs? Dobbs was in Catering and hardly in a position to jeopardize any intelligence operation. The idea was ridiculous and I put out of my mind any thought that the man to whose sick-bed I was bringing a little good cheer could possibly be regarded as a security risk.

Dobbs was in low spirits when I saw him. He had been the victim of a hit-and-run driver as he cycled home from the tube station at Muswell Hill. The car had come at him round a bend on the wrong side of the road. Both front and back offside wheels of the vehicle had run over – and crushed – his handlebars. The bicycle was a write-off, and in the circumstances Dobbs was lucky to escape with only the minor injuries he had sustained. To perk him up, I told him of my adventures of the night before. I knew the story would go no further. He smiled his approval of my quick-thinking action to put right the problem of the felled safe drop, but when I came to describe my confrontation with the stranger, his mouth fell open in amazement. Although I omitted one or two details of the episode in the version I told Dobbs, he was struck all the same by the curious nature of the event.

When the man sprang out of the shadows with a roar, I am afraid I let out a squeak of terror. I sat down on the damp earth and blinked up at the figure that swayed above me.

'Where the hell is it, then?'

'What?' I gasped. In the gloom I could make out nothing of the stranger's face, but he looked large and useful, and according to the Byfleet manual he was definitely in the position of dominant assailant to my low-guard prone attackee. The words of Sergeant Amsden flashed across my mind: 'When you hit, hit to hurt; if in doubt, talk them out.' I was in no position to hit or hurt, so I tried to diffuse the dangerous atmosphere with words. Also I was in no mood for a tussle.

'Filthy weather,' I said, furious with the quaver in my voice which might have betrayed my nervousness to a possible enemy. The shock of his sudden materialization from the surrounding night had left me trembling and I knew that if I tried to stand now, my knees could not be depended upon. As a matter of fact, I had never been so startled since the morning I had let myself into the office and Raymond Gray had jumped up from behind my desk with a Brillo pad on his head and a ping-pong ball wedged in his eye like a monocle, screaming, 'I'm Agnes and I'm yours!' I had dropped the bulky file of papers I was carrying, and without the restraint of an adequate number of paper-clips the documents had scattered themselves about the floor in a hopeless mess. Gray had apologized and helped me to pick up the papers, which had only resulted in making the confusion worse, the outcome being that the Dingbats had to wait till next day for W Sector's report on monthly consumption of carbon paper. I had to carry the can for that one.

'Still, what can you expect at this time of year,' I went on, trying to control my tremulous speech, 'I gather there's a depression over the Azores, or an isobar or something, and –'

'Where's my bloody passport?' shouted the figure as he swayed in the darkness above me, and I saw that he held a bottle of clear liquid in his hand, two-thirds empty, probably vodka.

'Your what?' I inquired, testing him. Clearly he knew something.

'My passport,' he repeated, sitting down heavily beside me. 'That's P, A, double arse, P, O, Ort.' He slung an arm round my shoulder and put his face close to mine – I was right about the vodka – and took my chin in his hand. 'You're my only friend, you know that?' he mumbled. 'You know that, don't you? My only friend.' For a dreadful moment I thought he was going to cry. I said nothing. 'So please tell me, my friend – you are my friend aren't you? 'Course you are. I'm your friend too, you know. I am. Yes, I'm your friend, so please, tell your friend, where's my . . . my . . . whatsaname . . .' He took a long swig from the bottle, then suddenly yelled at me. 'I want my *passport.*'

'Hush,' I whispered, with more authority than, in all conscience, I felt I possessed. 'Your passport is where you expected to find it.' For all I knew I was being set up, and I was loath to divulge any more to the stranger than I considered necessary. If he didn't know the location of the safe drop, I was damned if I was going to tell him.

He looked at me closely for a moment – why I cannot imagine, as it was far too dark for us to make out the details of one another's faces – and suddenly let out a great guffaw.

'The tree!' he shouted. 'It's in the bloody tree. Where's the tree? Tree? Tree? Where are you? Nice tree, where are you?'

Alarmed at the disturbance he was causing – there were houses near by, and this was supposed to be a clandestine operation – I began struggling to my feet. The man planted his hand on the top of my head and thrust himself into a standing position. Regaining my balance I looked up to find him looming unsteadily over me. The headlamps of a car passing down the lane that ran behind the terrace of houses that backed on to the waste ground swept across the scrubby terrain and briefly illuminated the stump with the white cross on it, rising at an angle from the trampled earth. With a wild wave of his bottle – I thought it wise to duck – the stranger let out a triumphant bellow and set off at a run in its direction. He had taken two unsteady paces before his leg caught the dog's lead. My view of what happened next was obscured, as the dog had been licking the lenses of my spectacles, but I suddenly saw Pongo's face take on a look of surprise and disappear rapidly backwards with a strangled yelp. Dimly I saw the man's black shape stumble forward into the tree, tree and man crashing to the ground with a winded oath. I rolled on to all fours, to the surprise of the already terrified dog who leaped sideways into the gorse.

I could now make out that the man was on his knees with one hand in the hollow at the top of the felled trunk. His cries of elation changed to a howl of despair.

'It's stuck!' he screamed. 'My passport's stuck! My bloody hand's stuck in this bloody tree.'

I threw myself at the tree, bringing the man down with a thump. Behind us the dog was thrashing in a panic and howling with torment, tangled by his lead in the prickly bushes.

'Quiet, Pongo!' I called, desperate and by now unsure how to stabilize the situation. The man writhed and kicked at the tree, trying to free his hand which grasped the passport. I clung to the other end of the trunk, quite sure that if I let go, the man who was possessed of the strength granted only to lunatics and drunks would, unrestrained, whirl the log round and round his head like a battle club, wreaking who knows what havoc.

'My fucking hand's jammed in this fucking tree,' he

screamed, 'let go, you stupid bastard, I want my passport.' As he yelled and writhed about and the dog created an unholy din among the gorse, lights began to appear in the house windows overlooking the scene.

I flung myself clear, stood up and spoke in a commanding tone. 'Now look here,' I said, 'this is very poor security procedure.'

My words must have had some effect. The man ceased his struggles and began to sob. I can, however, take no credit for the fact that, at the same moment, Pongo tore his lead free from the undergrowth and made for home. As the distraught animal skittered across the mud, each leg striving to propel it in a different direction, the man with the tree on his fist saw it. He ceased his sobbing and leapt to his feet. With a blood-curdling cry, he tore the tree-trunk free of the ground to defend himself and swung it towards the dog slithering in his direction. The end of the stump caught Pongo across the hindquarters, spinning him into a bewildered heap.

Pongo pulled himself together, co-ordinated his legs, and vanished. I later learned that he arrived home at the Crossed Keys in a very nervous state, and ever after that on walks, if anyone presented him with even a small log to fetch, he would flee howling in the opposite direction.

As I stood watching the dog disappear into the night, I heard a noise behind me. Turning into a crouch with a speed and smoothness that Byfleet's Sergeant Amsden would have remarked favourably upon, I saw the man blundering off through the undergrowth, the tree stump still jammed firmly on his fist. He paused to drain the bottle in his other hand, then flung it high towards the starry sky and was gone.

For a moment I stood alone, forcing deep breaths, staring up at the stars. The day's work was done. The passport was delivered to Smith. I could have wished for a smoother safe-drop operation, but it was over now and I was glad.

Helen was waiting up for me when I got home. She seemed a little beady as she surveyed the state of me.

'Fell over,' I explained, but that didn't help much.

The episode of Smith's passport was probably the most exciting field engagement that I was ever involved in. It happened on Thursday 24 May, 1951. I remember the date, however, not because of the impact which that event made upon me. I remember it because the next day, Friday 25 May, 1951, Sturgess and McBain defected.

Their precipitate and unexpected flight to Moscow had serious repercussions throughout the Foreign Office and all its Departments. The Duty Leave Roster was thrown into chaos. At this late date in May, when the wheeling and dealing for leave allocation was thought to be over, two prime holiday periods were suddenly back on the market. McBain's August leave, during the school holidays, was fought over vigorously by those Department members with a family, and Dawking of Stationery was fortunate enough to get it. Sturgess, on the other hand, had booked a free period in early June, a prime time for those without children, and Helen and I had high hopes of bringing forward our Skegness trip from November to the warm and hazy days of June. Our hopes were sadly dashed when the Head of NA Section did a covert deal with the Senior Leave Co-ordinator – G. E. D. Wainwright – and purchased the coveted June fortnight for himself and his flat-mate Rupert in exchange for a copy of the sheet music for the hit song 'Cry', autographed by Johnnie Ray for Wainwright's wife, who was said to be an awful woman. Bad feeling over this episode, once it had become common knowledge, persisted for some time. NA Section certainly had the cold shoulder from Records Division for several weeks. However, by the time Dobbs came back to work, the fuss had died down.

Nothing much of interest happened for some time. It was

five years before I was involved in field activities again. In the meantime, although speculation over the defection of Sturgess and McBain and the ensuing Leave Roster nonsense continued to be the subject of conversation at Department SRBs for a couple of months, business soon returned to normal. In MSI Section, Sector W, operations were conducted with greater efficiency than before, our paper-clip allocation having been put on a more realistic footing. My main concern during this period was the activation of a field-man in the Falkland Islands. As early as 1953 I had put forward my own personal feeling that the Falklands would become a thorn in our Department's flesh, and I predicted that, sooner or later, the Argentinians would cut up rough, although those were not the actual words I used in my memo. Many years later I was proved to be right, but at the time I had no idea how useful our Falklands field organization was to become.

It was not until July 1956 that I was to be, once again, involved in matters deep and dark and dangerous. The phone rang that summer's night, a night dank and tepid after the day's humid sunlight, as the clammy sheets clung to my pyjamas hours after I had retired to bed. Helen was still up. She was clearing away the glass and brandy bottle that had constituted her nightcap, consumed as I drained my cup of Nescafé. Perhaps that is the reason I was half-awake, a sudden whim having turned my normal desire for a bed-time Bournvita to a fancy for instant coffee. Whatever the reason for my wakefulness, I had the receiver to my ear before the phone had rung twice. Downstairs I could hear the clink and clatter of Helen in the kitchen as the voice spoke in my ear. It was the voice of Clive Black.

Black was Elsdon's assistant. Acting Deputy Controller in Chief of MSI. Although it was well past eleven o'clock, I was suddenly alert. Black required me to meet him next day at a distant safe address. A hotel. He said it was a matter of some importance. Discussion was imperative. He was not prepared to say any more on the phone, only to urge my presence at the meeting and to make sure I covered my tracks. Next day, after careful preparation, I made my own way to the rendezvous. I covered my tracks.

Six

The girl's scream snapped my mind to attention. I had been sitting at my desk the day after Black's telephone call. A casual observer glancing through the door would have seen me comfortably perched in the office chair, idly straightening the pencils and lining up the pad of code-sheets with the gilt line around the edge of the leather desk top, much the same as any other morning. On this occasion, however, my brain was working rapidly, making preparation for the meeting with Black. 'Cover your tracks,' he had said, and the phrase itself was enough to put me on the alert. Normally the instructions for a clandestine meeting would contain the words 'keep it quiet'. It would then be standard procedure to notify a Department colleague of the proposed meeting so that he could provide cover should the need arise. The code phrase 'cover your tracks' indicated that the mission was to be kept absolutely secret, even from the Department itself. I took this to mean that Black wanted to see me on some matter of high internal security, and accordingly began to plan my actions with great care. I had most of the details straight in my mind and was just working out my itinerary when the sudden scream abruptly uncoupled my train of thought.

I sat for a few moments, waiting for further sounds of disturbance. A distant door slammed. I could hear no voices, but then there came a faint scraping at my door and a ragged gasping sound. I had no wish to get involved in whatever was going on, but thought it my duty to find out what was making those curious noises. I crossed silently to the door and opened it swiftly. A body fell heavily into my arms.

The girl couldn't have been more than twenty. Her name was Carol Moon and she had been taken on as an Auntie some three weeks before.

'I'm sorry, I'm so sorry,' she sobbed, pushing away from me. 'I was leaning against your door. I'm so sorry.'

She sniffed loudly, and I saw the tears in her eyes and the dark tracks of mascara running downward through her make-up.

'Now, now,' I said, 'what's all this?'

'I didn't mean to disturb you, I'm so sorry,' and she began to weep again, great shuddering sobs as she pressed her head to my shoulder. I pushed her gently away.

'Here, here,' I said in a kind voice, 'this won't do at all now, will it?' Taking the handkerchief from my sleeve I rubbed at the moist powder smudge on my lapel. 'Now, what's been going on?' The girl stopped crying, which was a relief. The noise could have attracted attention and I flinched at the thought of what Raymond Gray would have made of it, had he caught me with a weeping Auntie on my shoulder. The girl looked up at me with a woebegone face and attempted a smile. The result was ghastly. She wore a short-sleeved white Angora wool jumper and close-fitting pants which finished half way down her calf. The clothes revealed the outline of her body in a way that could have been most distracting.

'It was Miss Muir,' she muttered.

'Oh, what's Agnes been up to? Given you the sharp edge of her tongue? Well, you mustn't mind old Agnes. She's a good sort underneath.'

'She . . . touched me.'

'Oh yes?' I said, carefully.

'She tried to put her hand inside my jumper.'

I turned away and cleared my throat. The girl would require careful handling.

'No,' I began, 'no, I don't think she did.'

'She tried.'

'No. It's Carol, isn't it? Well, Carol, I think you're mistaken. Miss Muir probably likes her Aunties to look smart. I expect she was simply trying to straighten your clothes.'

'That's not what it felt like,' she pouted. 'And what she said . . .'

'What did she say, Carol?'

'She said I had a juicy pair.'

The girl looked me straight in the eye as she spoke and I felt myself colouring like a schoolboy. I searched for the right words. I had to say something. Something polite. 'Ah well,' I remarked, 'and so you have. They're . . . excellent.' It was the girl's turn to blush and turn away her eyes. 'You see, Agnes was only paying you a compliment. Oh, she's a little rough and ready in her ways, but she's a good old stick.'

Carol turned towards me again. Now she was smiling properly. 'She really is a good old stick,' I repeated, and was reassured by her laughter. In spite of the ravaged make-up, her round little shop-girl's face was pretty in a sort of way. Her figure was full, with a plump, firm youthfulness. In ten years time she would be soft and fat, the make-up thicker, harsher; the sleek blonde hair dry and thin like spun sugar. For a moment as she looked up at me with damp brown eyes she reminded me of the young Helen.

'I'm sorry,' she said, seeming to be stifling a giggle, 'I'd better be going.' I felt a kind of release, such as I imagine a priest must feel after coping with an especially ticklish confession. I placed a hand on the top of her head.

'I'd better be going too,' I told her. 'I must be off to Leicester. A sickly aunt.'

She smiled again and kissed me lightly on the point of the chin. Then she was gone. It was a tender moment. One that I was later to remember.

After the girl had left, my thoughts eventually returned

to the 'cover-tracks' meeting with Black. I could not imagine why he wanted to see me. There had been a bit of a flap over the Sparrows requesting more pay for typing confidential reports with two carbons as opposed to one, but that particular situation had been prevented from reaching its flashpoint by the sure and swift actions of Penfold and von Swannenberg of Stationery. In any case, my own involvement with Stationery at this time was limited to occasional favours when the regular staff – depleted through personnel secondments to Dispatch and China Section – needed a helping hand. Apart from that, and some inter-Departmental nonsense over Suez and the Russian protective manoeuvres in Hungary, there was nothing in the daily memos that seemed to warrant Black's concern, or so it seemed to me. With the benefit of hindsight, I was later to realize that there was something.

At about this time the Government had issued a White Paper on the Sturgess and McBain scandal. Raymond Gray had laughed about it for days. I had tried to read it myself but had found it impenetrably boring, and not at all amusing, although Gray's reaction had set me looking very hard for the jokes. I found none and concluded that I had been correct in thinking Gray's sense of humour was not one universally shared in the Department. Shortly afterwards, however, the MP Marcus Lipton had asked a question in the House regarding Jim Phibley's involvement in the defection. This caused quite a flutter in the Department, especially among those who had hitched their wagons to Phibley's rising star; he was after all being tipped as next Head of MI6 after the retirement of Sir Lucius Carey.*

It must be some indication of the devious workings of the collective Department mind that this question in the House

* This is my pseudonym for the Head of MI6 at the time, who was not of course therefore related to Lucius Carey, Viscount Falkland, treasurer to the navy in 1690 when the explorer Captain John Strong named the Falkland Islands after him.

gave birth to a rumour. 'No smoke without fire,' remarked Agnes, among others, and the rumour grew. At Stockwell we had learned to live with rumour. In a game where hard facts are rare and not easy to come by, we develop the instinct to collate and interpret the nod and the wink and the whisper. And the rumour. On a dull winter's morning I have often contemplated the sight of Section personnel huddled against the wind that tugged at the skirts of their overcoats as they progressed in a monkish file towards the building at eight forty-five, each heading for a cell-like office where, like me, they would spend their day alone and in silence, confronting the latest rumour which had arisen to challenge their faith. Were the CIA in Argentina with us or against us? Had Interpol been infiltrated by the Israeli Secret Service? Was Jim Phibley the Third Man?

That particular question was soon to be answered in the House by the Prime Minister of the day – whom I shall refer to as Harold M* – who exonerated Phibley, to the satisfaction of myself at least. Later I was to be proved wrong. I cannot confess to having had any misgivings at the time and even Black's telephone call did not set the alarm bells jangling in my mind.

Black had asked me to meet him in Banbury. By six o'clock that evening I was to present myself in the bar of the Whately Hall Hotel and to wait for him to join me. Before leaving home, I had telephoned the hotel to book a room for the night. At the office I had made my plans for the trip, but the incident with Carol Moon had set back my timetable, so that it was past eleven, after she had left my office, that I began the operation in earnest.

I buzzed my secretary on the intercom, to tell her I would be away for a day or so. There was no reply. Peeping into her cubicle I discovered that there was no one there, the typewriter cowled and silent, the nail-polish and make-up neatly marshalled by the pile of romantic novels. I called

* Later Sir Harold M.

the secretarial pool on the internal phone system – newly installed on Elsdon's insistence – and at the third attempt got through. The girl at the pool informed me that my secretary had been temporarily requisitioned to help with the back-log of congratulatory mail to be sent to Department members who had been recognized in the New Year's Honours List. On my insistence she agreed to lend me a temporary secretary on a short-term basis, and eventually I was put on to a girl called Dilys Barker, who had once been an Auntie but had chosen to revert to the post of secretary rather than endure the rule of Agnes. Dilys asked what I needed. I took the opportunity to cover my tracks by telling her that it was all right, I didn't need anything, as I would be away for a couple of days in Leicester, visiting an aunt who was sick. Dilys made a puzzled noise and hung up, but she would remember my story.

Next I made my way to Bill Elsdon's office. He was not there, but I told his secretary to give him the message that I had been unexpectedly called away for a day or two, to Leicester, to visit an ailing relative. To make sure that the information got through, I left a personal memo on his desk.

TO: HEAD MSI SECTION
FROM HEAD MSI/W SECTION
(PERSONAL)
Gone to Leicester. Aunt sick. Back day after tomorrow.
Signed, Geoffrey T. Alsop

As I left Elsdon's office, I bumped into Agnes.

'Hello,' she said, 'what are you up to? Carrying tales to teacher?'

My cover was well established in my mind and her sudden appearance did not disconcert me. I replied without a single involuntary facial movement:

'Oh, just leaving a memo for the old man. Thought I'd better. Going to Leicester actually. You won't see me for a couple of days. Aunt of mine, not very well. Lives in Leicester.

Yes, I'm going to see her. Just for a day or so, till she's better. Thought I ought to go, though. To Leicester. See the old aunt. Her name's Walsh. Hilda Walsh. Eighty-six. Marvellous really. Lived in Leicester all her life. She's there now. Not very well, so I'm going to see her.'

'Fine,' said Agnes cheerfully, 'see you when you get back then. From Leicester.' With a wolfish grin, she slipped into Elsdon's office.

After collecting my things I popped in to see Raymond Gray and give him my cover story, but I was told he was out on the job, working on something hot, so I told his personal assistant about my aunt in Leicester and trotted down the stairs to the street. For July it was an unexpectedly warm day and so I carried the blue overcoat over my arm. As I left the building the duty Security Officer remarked that it was a scorcher.

'Certainly warm,' I replied, 'but I dare say it's warmer in Leicester. I'm going there as a matter of fact, just for a couple of days. To see a sick aunt.'

I crossed the road to the phone-box opposite and called Helen. This was not a call it would have been wise for me to make from inside headquarters. The ringing tone went on for some time before I heard the receiver picked up and pressed button A. Helen sounded a little out of breath and I commented on it.

'Oh. Yes,' she panted, 'I had to run for the phone.' She must have had the wireless on, as I could hear it murmuring softly behind her.

'I thought you'd still be in bed,' I said, 'thought you'd take it in the bedroom.'

'I'm not taking it in the bedroom, Geoffrey, it's after eleven-thirty. Of course I'm not in the bedroom.'

'Where are you?'

'I'm in the kitchen. That's why I had to run to answer the phone.'

'We don't have a phone in the kitchen.'

'I mean hall. I'm standing in the hall. And I've got my clothes on.'

'Good. Helen, I want you to remember something. If anyone from the office phones, say I've gone to my sick aunt in Leicester.'

'I didn't know you had an aunt in Leicester.'

'I haven't, but that's what you must tell them.'

There was a pause, and Helen seemed to be fiddling with the volume knob on the radio.

'Sorry, Geoffrey, yes,' she resumed, 'you've gone out with your aunt from Leicester.'

'No. I've gone to Leicester to see her.'

'But you just said you haven't got an aunt in Leicester.'

'I know. It's a cover.'

'Oh, I see. Why are you going to Leicester, then?'

'I'm not going to Leicester. I'm going somewhere else.'

'Where?'

'I can't tell you.'

'Why not? What's so secret about where your aunt lives?'

'I'm not going to see my aunt.'

'I don't understand,' Helen complained, then with a flash of interest so rare at that early hour, 'are you up to something?'

'Yes,' I said, 'I'm up to something, and I don't want anybody to know about it. If anyone phones, just tell them I've gone to visit my sick aunt in Leicester.'

'Yes, of course,' said Helen. 'Will you be away tonight, then?'

'Yes, my pie.'

'All night?'

'All night.'

'Not in Leicester?'

'No.'

'But away all night?'

'Helen, this is for your ears only. Do you understand? I shall not be in Leicester, but I shall be away all night.'

'Good.'

'What do you mean, "Good"?'

'I mean I understand, Geoffrey. And that's good, isn't it?'

'Yes, Helen, it's good you understand.'

'Good,' she said brightly and I heaved a sigh of relief.

I hung up the phone and left the call-box. As I made my way towards Clitheroe Road and the car I glanced across at the Headquarters Building and softly swore at what I saw. Most of the windows were blank, their venetian blinds closed against the sunlight, except for one, and in that one I saw Agnes staring down at me. Even at that distance I could sense the malevolence in her eye. Now she would be wondering what call it was that had to be made from a public call-box and not from the telephone on my office desk. I pretended I had not seen her and set off towards the car. As I walked along I slapped my thigh and scratched my head and made laughing movements, as a man might do who had left his office, then remembered an important phone-call and decided to use a public call-box rather than go all the way back to the office telephone. I shrugged a good deal and behaved as if the whole business were utterly unimportant. Halfway down Clitheroe Road I turned abruptly and hurried back to the phone-box. There I picked up the briefcase I had inadvertently left behind which contained the cheddar and Branston sandwiches I had earlier prepared for my lunch, and made my way back to the car. Agnes was still at the window. I didn't bother to shrug this time. I felt I had made my point, and it hurt my neck.

I drove to King's Cross Station. There I purchased a return ticket to Leicester and paid by cheque, complaining as I did so about the price of rail travel these days, so that they would remember me. Returning to the car, I then drove to Camden Town, and at a Red Cross shop bought a battered second-hand suitcase, into which I transferred my toilet bag, pyjamas, dressing gown, slippers, clean underwear and sandwiches. Having parked the car in a dreary side street, I carried my suitcase to a nearby Godfrey Davis car hire company and rented a Ford Anglia for a few days, as I explained, to visit an indisposed aunt in Leicester.

By one o'clock I was on the road. At five past two the A6 had taken me to Harpenden. There I left the car in a pub car park and caught a suburban line train to Luton. The Godfrey Davis branch in Luton rented me a Ford Zephyr, and I made my way across country towards Oxfordshire, driving at a steady fifteen miles per hour to make sure I wasn't being followed. When a police car crept up behind me and sat on my tail I accelerated to thirty mph, and once the inquisitive officers had turned off at Leighton Buzzard I began my tortuous route towards Banbury. Down the Aylesbury Road to Wing, then right to Cublington and Dunton; Hoggeston to Steeple Claydon, South to Edgcott, then Marsh Gibbon; Stratton Audley, Fringford, Hethe and Baynards Green to Barley Mow; north to Hinton-in-the-Hedges, north again to Farthinghoe; bearing right to Monckton Pinkeney, west to Lower Boddington; Fenny Compton, Avon Dassett, Shotteswell and Warmington; there I stopped to ask directions, and found I wasn't as far from Banbury as I had feared.

At five forty-five I was standing, suitcase in hand, by the reception desk in the Whately Hall Hotel. It was my intention to sign in under an assumed name. In a normal field operation it is never left to the agent to choose his own cover-name – a precaution that became standard practice after the 1946 Paris incident – as the Department likes to have a record of exactly who is operating where under what name at any given time. So it is that the Bedmakers issue a monthly list to all personnel indicating his or her choice of available covers. However, this being a cover-tracks assignment, I had decided to make use of a personal non-attributable AKA.* The field-name I had selected for the Banbury assignment was Derek Savage.

* AKA = Also Known As.

'Your name, please sir,' smiled the attractive receptionist.

'Der . . .' I began, then stopped. Suddenly I felt flustered, for out of the corner of my eye I had caught sight of the second-hand suitcase in my hand. On the battered leather of the lid facing the receptionist were stamped the faint but unmistakable initials RR.

'Der . . . er . . . Rogers,' I stammered.

'And your full name, Mr Rogers?'

'Roy,' I said. The name came to me from nowhere, and I was sorry the moment I uttered it.

'Mr Roy Rogers,' she smiled.

'That's me,' I agreed.

The girl filled in the rest of the details in the book and called a porter.

'Will you see Mr Roy Rogers to his room,' she said loudly, 'room 303.'

Several heads turned as I walked towards the lift, feeling rather pink, and on the way up to the third floor the young porter made some silly remark about saddlebags.

Seven

In room 303 I unpacked and washed and regained my composure. Black had asked me to meet him at six o'clock, and it was only one minute past the hour when I stepped out of the lift downstairs and strolled casually past reception to the bar. I leaned on the counter in a relaxed sort of way, ignoring the cries of 'Yipee!' and 'Yahoo!' from rather a noisy crowd in one corner.

'What'll it be, partner?' inquired the barman, 'three fingers of rye?'

'A small gin and it,' I replied coolly, and retreated to a table screened by a partition. The man brought the drink over, and a bowl of peanuts, and asked if I would like a nose-bag for Silver.

'Trigger!' shouted one of the group in the corner who had been listening to our exchange. His companions laughed uproariously and the barman had a good old chuckle. I said, 'No, thank you,' and sipped my drink in silence.

At seven-thirty Black had still not put in an appearance. I had consumed several peanuts, two gin and its, and was now prudently confining myself to a neat it. The noisy people had left the corner and gone into the dining-room, and the bar was quiet. I went up to the barman and inquired if anyone had been asking for me. He shook his head. I left the bar and approached the reception desk. Behind me the barman carried on cleaning a pair of bakelite ashtrays, and I am sure it was no accident that he was making clippety-clop sounds with them.

'I was wondering, has anybody been trying to contact me?' I asked the receptionist, who smiled.

'No, Mr Rogers, nobody.'

Then of course I realized that Black, not knowing my last-minute change of field-name, would not have been asking for Roy Rogers. As a matter of fact we had not discussed the question of cover at all, and he would therefore have no idea of my assumed identity, just as I had no idea of his. Our contact would have to be visual, but as he was already over ninety-five minutes late I wondered if something had delayed him and he had therefore tried to get in touch with me. The problem facing me was how to find out if he had.

'I was wondering, then,' I asked the girl in a very offhand way, as if it were quite unimportant, 'if anybody has been trying to contact . . . anybody else.'

'I don't understand, I'm afraid, Mr Rogers.'

'Any messages. For anybody. Anybody with a different name.'

'Not Rogers?'

'No. Not that it matters. I just sort of wondered.'

'Well, there's a message for Miss Mottram.'

'Is there? Is there really. Well well.' I doubted very much if Black would have assumed that I was operating under the name of Miss Mottram.

'Were you expecting to meet someone, Mr Rogers?'

'Yes, a Mr Bl . . . a man.'

'What's his name? I can have him paged.'

'No no, no need. If he's around I'll know him when I see him.'

'What does he look like? Then if he turns up I can direct him to you.'

It would do no harm to describe Black to the girl, who was trying hard to be helpful.

'Well, the man who is supposed to be meeting me is rather short, skinny, well . . . thinnish frame. Longish hair.

Black greasy hair. No, not so much greasy as slick. Slick black longish hair. And a small moustache.'

'Oh yes,' replied the receptionist with a glint of recognition, 'looks like a weasel.'

'A bit. Slightly weaselish.'

'Pointy nose, shifty little eyes?'

'Pointed nose, yes. The eyes are sort of alert and probing. Intelligent.'

'But shifty?'

'Mm . . .'

'He's in the dining-room. I'll have him called.'

I returned to my secluded table in the bar. A few moments later I was joined by a shifty little chap who did look remarkably like a weasel. He was not Clive Black. He was a man from the party in the corner, the one who had shouted 'Trigger!'

'Hello, old sport,' he exclaimed, shaking me limply by the hand. 'Trevor Mouldman. Pleased to meet you, Roy. I'm travelling in ladies' underwear.' He laughed loudly.

I nodded and smiled. 'I'm Mr Rogers,' I explained, and he gurgled with mirth.

'A word to the wise,' he chuckled, leaning very close to me so that tiny moist particles of his dinner sprayed from his lips on to my cheek. 'If I were you, I'd change that monnicker of yours. I mean, it's too good a chance to miss for fellows who like a bit of fun, and it's only good-natured banter after all, but I dare say it gets right on your tits. Be honest, it does, doesn't it? Eh? Roy Rogers?' He guffawed again, dislodging a large morsel of vegetable matter which landed on my tie. It may have been swede.

Half an hour later I realized Mr Mouldman was going to stick to me for the rest of the evening. When they emerged from the dining-room, he called over his cronies who joined us and kept up a constant stream of cowboy references. Two of them had a mock gun-fight in the middle of the bar, and one fell over against the table, throwing a half-full glass of lager into my lap.

Black never appeared. By nine o'clock I was beginning to wonder if my elaborate track-covering manoeuvre had been worthwhile after all. My companions were getting drunker and noisier, and Mouldman had told me rather a nasty joke about a little boy and his grandmother at least three times, and I still didn't get it. I had a great deal on my mind. Half way through their fourth rendering of 'Home on the Range' I was relieved to feel a gentle tap on my shoulder. It was the receptionist.

'Mr Alsop? MI6?' she inquired.

'Ah . . .' I ventured.

'I thought it must be you. There's a message for you from a Mr Elsdon. He would like you to lunch with him tomorrow. At the Reform Club. He said it was most important.'

How Elsdon had learned of my whereabouts I was never to discover. However, my cover was blown, and one thing was clear; Black would not be appearing that night. Bidding Mr Mouldman and his friends a hasty goodnight, I checked out of the hotel and drove back to London by a more direct route than the one by which I had come.* I left the hired car at the Godfrey Davis depot at Euston, took a taxi to my own car at King's Cross, and drove home to arrive shortly after eleven.

I was surprised to find Helen still up when I entered the lounge. She lay on the sofa in the black nylon négligé with flame trimmings which she very seldom wore. Poor Helen was quite startled by my entrance. She had not expected me home that night. I kissed her warmly on the shoulder and remarked on the négligé.

'Oh, I was feeling rather hot,' she explained.

Both bars of the fire were glowing orange, the lights were

* Down the A41 to Adderbury then to Oxford on the A432 where I joined the A40 to London.

dimmed, and gentle music played on the radiogram tuned to the Light Programme.

'You've certainly made yourself very snug,' I remarked, sinking on to the pouffe.

'Yes. Actually I think I'm a bit too hot. It's given me a headache.'

She did look rather flushed. A sheen of perspiration glistened through the powder on her upper lip, and her hand trembled as she set down the brandy glass on the occasional table beside her.

'You look ready for bed,' I remarked.

'I only put it on because I felt hot, Geoffrey.'

'Up the wooden stairs to Bedfordshire with you, young lady.'

'Goodnight, Geoffrey.'

'Goodnight, my pet. Sweet dreams. I shall be up shortly.'

'I'm so sorry about this beastly headache. Oh, how was your aunt?'

'Goodnight, Helen.'

'Goodnight.'

It was not long before I joined her in the bedroom. The light was out, but Helen was not asleep. As I lay beside her, going over the day's events again and again in my mind and trying to make the connections which eluded me, I was aware of her tossing and turning beside me. Why had Black failed to appear? A cover-tracks meeting was a serious business, and Black a conscientious agent. Why had he wished to see me under such rigorous conditions of security? How had Elsdon known where to find me? Why did he wish me to join him for lunch?

My mind still reluctant to let go of the problems that obsessed me, I had fallen into a fitful doze when the doorbell rang. Three short bursts, a pause, then one long one. The alarm clock told me that it was a quarter past midnight. I got out of bed, dashed if I was going to drag myself downstairs to open the front door at that time of night. I pulled up the sash window, which opened about two inches, then stuck – Helen had been on at me for weeks about easing it – and tried to peep out. Outside it was pitch dark and I could see nothing.

'Who's there?' I called through the crack. There was no reply, but I thought I heard a scuffling, and then a dustbin clattered to the ground. Turning back to the bed, I saw that Helen was sitting bolt upright. I reassured her, knowing her fears of midnight prowlers, and by the time I had snuggled myself cosily between the sheets again she was fast asleep. Repose did not come to me swiftly, and as I lay there awaiting slumber I heard a distant car door slam and the sound of its engine roaring off into the night.

Helen was up bright and early next morning. She came downstairs as I was about to leave the house at eleven-thirty. I had decided that, having established the sick aunt in Leicester story so successfully, it would be pointless to turn up at the office before the afternoon. Not only would it be a waste of some pretty useful cover work, but it would also invite a lot of unnecessary inquiries into why my aunt had made so rapid a recovery. Also, as my first engagement for the day was lunch with Bill Elsdon, I didn't see why I couldn't just this once take the morning off.

As I pecked Helen goodbye at the front door, the telephone rang. It was Dennis Dobbs, and he seemed in a very queer state of mind indeed. He had been in and out of hospital for some time – he had not yet returned to active service – and what he told me gave me cause to question the balance of his reason. The call was made through the operator from a public call-box. When I asked where he was he wouldn't say, but maintained that this method of contact was necessary as he had reason to believe, as he put it, that his own telephone had been tapped. Naturally I took this cock and bull story with a pinch of salt. As it turned out, that was not the only thing he had phoned to tell me about. I listened with growing concern as he went on to explain about the milk. As his story unfurled I became more and more convinced that his old cycling accident had in some way unhinged his mind. According to Dobbs, someone was making an attempt on his life. He claimed that he had noticed unusual perforations in the foil caps of the milk bottles on his doorstep that morning. He had thought no more of it until he sat down to breakfast and poured the milk on to his cereal. If I was to believe his story, Dobbs had looked on in horror as his Grape-Nuts dissolved.

Author's Note

As my co-writer and I reached this point in the manuscript during its preparation for publication, we received a memo from our publisher's Legal Department. They had been sounding out the Foreign Office's attitude towards the security aspects of certain revelations contained in this book, and were delighted to hear that the publisher's formal 'need to know' had been granted an official 'couldn't care less'.

Therefore at this point it can be revealed that – as the more astute reader may already have suspected – several of the characters central to this story are indeed Guy Burgess, Donald Maclean, Kim Philby and Sir Anthony Blunt.

Although the identities of others mentioned must still remain concealed, from this point onwards we shall refer to these four by their real names. Time being short, however, and having got this far, we the writers decided it was not worth revising the first part of the book and changing all the references to these names, which would have been an awfully fiddly business.

G.T.A.

Eight

It had been five years since the man in the Gents' at Stockwell had advised me to keep an eye on Dobbs. Nevertheless the incident had remained teasingly in a corner of my memory, and in the light of Dobbs' increasingly eccentric behaviour I was beginning to wonder if he was indeed a potential security risk of the sort that merited covert surveillance. For the time being I decided to do no more than the stranger had suggested; to keep an eye on him myself rather than turn him over to the Bird-Watchers for D-level observation. After all, Dobbs was my friend, although we were never close. Years later, when the dust began to settle after the Seventh Man revelations had thrown the Department into that flurry of confusion and suspicion that became known as the Dark Ages, there were those who said that my handling of the Dobbs business had been misguided, and there were others who agreed.

All thought of Dobbs vanished from my mind as I mounted the flight of steps leading from Pall Mall to the massive hall of the Reform Club. I had never been inside the building before, and my first reaction was one of awe. Our house would have fitted comfortably into the great room and still have left space for the members to mingle around the colonnaded periphery. Huge marble pillars rose from the mosaic floor to support a grand gallery, and towered beyond it to the distant vault of the ceiling. Several men, some of whose faces were vaguely familiar to me from the newspapers, stood around in small groups, holding drinks they had purchased from a large white-draped table half-hidden behind two of the pillars. Elsdon was nowhere to be seen, and I wandered in a little circle for a few moments trying to spot him in one of the darker corners.

A loud cry of 'Hello' caused me and everyone else to look up. Elsdon was leaning over the stone balustrade around the gallery, waving his handkerchief. I waved back, feeling a little selfconscious as I did so. I knew that many of the gentlemen's clubs had curious rules and I was unsure about the etiquette of non-members waving in the hall. The gaze of the others now focused upon me as I made my way to the staircase across the intricate designs of polished marble, wishing that I had chosen to wear my brown shoes that morning, as they were the ones that didn't squeak.

Set around the gallery were several small tables with comfortable-looking leather chairs. Elsdon stood beside one of them chatting to a tall, delicately-featured man with a fine head of grey hair. Elsdon greeted me cheerfully and introduced his companion. I shook hands with Sir Anthony Blunt.

Blunt apologized for the fact that he had a pressing engagement at his own club – the Travellers – and after thanking Elsdon for the drink, he left us. We sat, and Elsdon ordered drinks for us both, gin and it for me and a large pink gin for himself. He told me that his friend Sir Anthony was Keeper of the Queen's pictures and had recently received a knighthood for his services. It struck me that this was an unusually high distinction to be bestowed upon a picture-keeper, but kept my thoughts on the matter to myself.

It turned out that Elsdon and Blunt had been friends at Cambridge. They had stayed in touch ever since and often lunched together at one another's clubs. With a sudden smile Elsdon nodded towards our luxurious surroundings and observed that this was 'a far cry from the old CP sherry parties in some student's draughty rooms in Cambridge'. I replied that I imagined it was. Elsdon looked at me thoughtfully, and asked:

'What year were you up, then? Must have been, what, 1940, 41?'

'During the war I was in the RAF.'

When my call-up papers had come I had joined the air force. The grace and freedom of the planes I had seen wheeling through the heights had appealed to my then young and adventurous spirit. My heroes were the fighter pilots, the Brylcreem boys. During basic training I grew a handlebar moustache and spent hours memorizing the jargon – 'wizard crate', 'Ginger's bought it', 'Algy's pranged his kite' – and so it was that when the young knights of the air looped and whirled through the hot blue sky in what was to be remembered as the Battle of Britain, I was serving in Kent, doing my bit, manning an RAF telephone switchboard two hundred feet underground.

'So you didn't get up to the varsity until '45?' asked Elsdon.

'I'm afraid I didn't go to varsity.'

'What, neither of them?'

'No. I'm sorry.'

'Well which little CP cell did you belong to? Not one of those dreary Midlands outfits, full of workmen?'

'Actually, I never belonged to the Communist Party in my life.'

'Oh.' Elsdon raised his eyebrows. I may be many things, but I am not a fool, and I was beginning to resent the implications of my superior's questions. I was also somewhat put out at realizing how little of my background he seemed to know.

'I never went to Cambridge,' I said firmly, 'and I never served the Communist Party there or anywhere else. I realize that almost everyone else in the Department did, but I didn't, and I was not aware until now that it was a condition of employment.'

I thought I had put it rather well, but Elsdon laughed. 'Now, now, Geoffrey,' he said, patting my knee, 'no need to get out of your pram. I know you're a damned good type, whatever your background. And, I may say, our masters have been following your career with great interest. They consider you utterly solid.'

His flattery confused me and I mumbled something, half apology, half thanks.

'The reason I mentioned the old CP, Geoffrey, was just that I know you keep a photograph of that bod Lenin in your office.'

'Lenin?' I asked in surprise.*

'Yes. Thought he must be a hero of yours. Bit of a thinker, deep sort of bird, like you, Geoffrey.'

'That's a picture of Stalin.'

'No it isn't. Stalin had a big black moustache. Your fellow's a little chap with a beard and specs. Lenin.'

'I don't think it is. Still, if you say so I won't argue. Whoever it is, I keep his photograph so that whenever the need arises, I can look into the eyes of the enemy.'

'Very good, Geoffrey, very good.'

'Thank you, sir.'

Elsdon smiled broadly. 'Call me S,' he said.

Later I was to find out that both of us had been half right about the photograph. It was not Stalin, but nor was it Lenin. A few minutes' research in the *Reader's Digest Book of the People's Revolution* – borrowed from the coffee table of one of Helen's friends – revealed that the face on my office wall in fact belonged to Trotsky.†

The lunch was splendid. Elsdon studied the wine list for some time, saying that he felt it appropriate to the occasion that we should share a few glasses of something rather special. I suggested a bottle of Blue Nun, and saw that he was a little put out to discover that I had some small

* 'Lenin' was the cover-name of the Soviet Revolutionary leader Vladimir Ilyich Ulyanov.

† Trotsky was the cover-name used by the Soviet Revolutionist Lev Davidovich Bronstein.

knowledge of fine wines. In the end he chose a couple of bottles of something called Puligney Montrachet, which tasted quite nice although it wasn't very sweet.

As I expected, Elsdon did not get to the point until the brandies had been served. Between puffs at his Corona he began to edge the conversation round to what Raymond Gray would have called the gritty-nitty.

'You know,' he said, quite matter-of-factly, 'that Burgess and Maclean were both members of this club?'

'I didn't know,' I replied. 'How odd.'

'How, odd?'

'Well, odd that Russian spies should belong to a gentlemen's club in Pall Mall. Not somehow compatible with socialist principles, I should have thought.'

'My dear Geoffrey, what on earth do socialist principles have to do with it?'

'My dear S,' I responded expansively, 'surely their activities imply some sort of commitment to the other side's ideology.'

Elsdon threw back his head and laughed loud and long. I was taken aback by his reaction to my argument, but I joined in with his mirth. I knew my place.

'Dear dear Geoffrey, you really do make the most exquisite jokes. You're a very under-rated man, you know. A very very deeply under-rated man.'

'Thank you,' I said, flattered.

'My God, if they only knew.'

'If who only knew?'

'The people who under-rate you, Geoffrey. Almost everybody.' Elsdon slapped his open hand on the table and laughed until tears came to his eyes. I wasn't feeling quite so flattered now. Taking a breath, Elsdon noticed the expression on my face. He leaned forward rapidly and grasped my wrist. 'But there are those who do not underestimate you, Geoffrey. I admit I had trouble convincing them – I wasn't sure myself, you know – but convince them I did. Our masters know that you are worth your weight in gold. They trust you.'

I felt flattered again. Nonetheless I was beginning to suspect that Elsdon was playing some game with me and that it was my move.

'They trusted Burgess. And Maclean.'

'Well of course they did,' he sighed. 'Those two comedians are in Moscow now, you know. You'd think they'd be cold, they'd be safe there, no threat. But you know what they're going to do? They must be dotty. They're going to give a press conference. In Moscow. To the world press.'

Elsdon drained his glass and ordered two more. We sat in silence until the waiter had brought us our replenished snifters. Elsdon sighed.

'God knows what they'll say. They could put a lot of good people at risk.'

'Oh surely not after all this time. The Bed-makers and Face-savers must have covered all our field-men by now.'

'I don't think you understand me, Geoffrey. This matter is beyond the control of the Department's Peace-Artists. Our masters are very edgy over what Burgess and Maclean may reveal about our deep-penetration operations. My own position has become shall we say delicate. My choice of action may change from one moment to the next. I shall be vulnerable. I shall need support. If I am to play the shark I shall need my pilot fish. If I am to be the heavily-armoured, quick-tempered rhino I may avoid extinction at the hands of the hunters, but I shall need my secretary birds to pick off the parasites.'

'Yes, of course,' I joined in, getting the idea, 'and if you were the cheese in the trap, you would need your mouse.'

'No, that doesn't make sense, Geoffrey. What I am trying to say is that I need people at my back.'

'Daggers drawn!' I exclaimed in a dramatic voice.

'Not necessarily,' replied Elsdon, accidentally taking my glass of brandy and placing it behind the cruet. 'I just need to know that there are those on my side who will serve my interests. Our interests. The interests of our masters.'

'You can count on me, S.'

'Yes. Yes I know I can. You have already done me a small favour or two. I would only like your word that support in the future will be forthcoming. In affairs, I mean, where official Department channels may have to be bypassed.'

'Ah,' I said with a sly wink, 'are you by any chance referring to the business of Smith's passport?'

'That sort of thing, possibly, yes.'

'I'm your man.'

'Thank God!' exclaimed Elsdon, leaning back in his chair. The room seemed to swim before me as I realized for the first time what a lonely position S occupied as head of MSI Section, an autonomous cog in the great Department machine, yet unable even to trust his closest colleagues. Something in the way I was looking at him must have prompted Elsdon's next remark.

'There have been those who disappointed me. Are you all right?'

'Fine. Fine!'

The big man sighed, fixing me with a piercing yet ambivalent glare. 'Black has gone,' he said in an uncharacteristically soft tone.

'Your deputy? Black?' Mention of the name reminded me of the odd events of the night before. Elsdon nodded sadly.

'The pressure of work was getting on top of him. He has been relieved of those responsibilities, posted as Head of Hospitality to Beirut. He left last night.'

The news came as a relief to me in three ways. First, it explained Black's non-appearance at the Banbury hotel. Second, Head of Hospitality was a much coveted posting. Third, because I knew that Beirut was used as a safe refuge for agents whose field-work had become too hot for comfort. It was common knowledge, for example, that the estimable

Kim Philby, temporarily suspended by Section on the strength of rumour alone, was currently working there as a foreign correspondent for the *Economist* and the *Observer*, biding his time and waiting for the fuss to die down, under as good a cover as I had ever heard of.

I nodded wisely and said I was pleased to hear it about Black, adding that it was clear to those of us with our fingers on the pulse that Black was not the only one crumbling under the pressure.

'Who else do you have in mind?' asked Elsdon, with a hunted look in his eyes.

'Dobbs,' I replied, dropping the name into the conversation like a pebble into a limpid pond.

'Oh, Dobbs? Yes. Dobbs has certainly gone peculiar. He has become dangerous, although God knows he makes precious little sense.'

I began to chuckle, then noticed the serious, almost pained look on Elsdon's face.

'I'm afraid,' he said with gravity, 'Dobbs' contract will have to be terminated with extreme prejudice.'

'An early retirement?'

'A capital settlement, I fear.'

I was sorry to hear that Dobbs was to be put out to grass, but it was clearly the only thing to be done. Taking my cue from Elsdon's mention of a capital settlement, I assured him that I was well aware of the inadequacy of a Department pension, and promised to organize an office whip-round to give Dobbs a good send-off.

After that Elsdon spoke little as he polished off his cigar and brandy and then, apparently lost in thought, drained my glass as well. He seemed to be his old self again by the time we split the bill and he saw me off into the street.

My afternoon at the office was spent pondering the partition of Cyprus. Because of its geographical location, one half of it came under my control as Head of MSI W Sector, the other half under Raymond Gray's E Sector.

Both of us knew that there were problems on the island, but it had taken us many months to agree upon security allocations. The fact that this took more than two years to rationalize has been cited by some as the reason why British involvement in that island was so disastrously inadequate. In our defence I can only point out the fact that the delicate negotiations between Sectors were not helped by Whitehall's constant imperative demands to know what the hell was going on. In any case, two weeks later Cyprus was taken over by M Section, and Gray and I affirmed to each other that we were well rid of it.

'Been there once,' said Gray. 'Nasty place. Very hot and rocky.'

Once the Cyprus dilemma had been taken off our hands, I contacted Dobbs. I offered to give him a game of golf at the weekend, but on the Saturday morning he cried off, having unaccountably contracted a case of bilharzia.

Nine

In spite of Bill Elsdon's worries, the Burgess and Maclean Moscow press conference raised no dust. The two men simply handed to the journalists a short prepared statement which contained precious little information apart from the assertion that although they had both been Communists since their Cambridge days, they had never been spies, which was, as Raymond Gray put it, a hoot. At the time, of course, there was no hard evidence against them, apart from their defection itself, but shortly after that damp squib of a press conference, Burgess revealed to Tom Driberg – the politician, journalist and bon viveur who was writing a book about Burgess for Weidenfeld and Nicolson – details of the botched Anglo-American attempts to topple the régime in Albania. In so doing the defector broke the Official Secrets Act, and became a wanted man in the United Kingdom. In those days, and at the time of writing, there was unfortunately no extradition agreement with the Soviet Union.

Things in MSI Section were pretty quiet for the next five years or so. Most of the Department activity during that period was concentrated in mainland Sections, Cuba having been taken out of our hands. SEA Section had a particularly tough time, I recall, trying to discover exactly what the Americans thought they were up to in Viet Nam. The conduct of the overt US campaign in that territory was so bizarre and inconsistent that it was generally assumed to be a diversionary tactic to distract attention from some other operation. Agnes dismissed the whole business as an election stunt which had got out of hand, and she may well have been right.

In 1962, however, there was a bit of an upset. All Section and Sector heads were called to an emergency meeting in the rarely used safe-house in Balham. There was a bit of ill-feeling when Miss Harley, Head of Photo-Copying Section, announced her intention to attend. Although she strictly-speaking qualified as a Section Head, that being after all her title, the newly formed Photo-Copying Section was really no more than a Division, like Stationery or Transport. Indeed the mis-naming of Photo-Copying as a Section had raised many a hackle among the operational staff, and I had drafted a stiff memo myself in opposition to this classification, although I never sent it.

I arrived early at the safe-house; 15, Thurleigh Crescent, Balham.* In the large, bleak upstairs room several men stood around the gas fire which hissed and popped in the black cast-iron grate. The brown linoleum was worn and scarred, and three rickety bentwood chairs were pushed back to the stained yellow walls. Dirty net curtains hung like cataracts in the fractured windows.

In the early sixties the psychologists had moved in to advise on the maximization of motivation among Department personnel. I had heard it on good authority that the safe-house had been chosen and the meeting-room decorated by the psychologists to reinforce the staff's perceived image of their calling. It was said that the curtains had been dyed to a specific shade of dismal grey, a mock Adam fireplace ripped out and replaced by the gas fire, the wallpaper stained and peeled, and the linoleum hand-distressed by experts. The effect was disturbingly oppressive.

The room slowly filled up with staff. I was pushed back to the wall by the door and had some difficulty in seeing

* For security reasons I have not given the exact address. It was not number fifteen, and the road was not called Thurleigh Crescent. Nor, as a matter of fact, was the house in Balham.

what was going on. I knew, however, that the group by the gas fire were very senior people indeed. Apart from Bill Elsdon and his opposite numbers from the other Sections, there were the Heads of MI5 and MI6, Chiefs of Military Security, and a Senior Officer from Scotland Yard. It was pointed out to me by Raymond Gray that there were three senior civil servants from Whitehall, and I recognized the face of a Cabinet Minister. My guess was that the meeting had been called to co-ordinate the introduction of metrication to our Departments, but I was wrong.

One of the Whitehall men opened the proceedings by clearing his throat.

'Ladies and gentlemen,' he began, the room subsiding into attentive silence, 'the cat, I'm afraid to say, is among the pigeons.'

Elsdon exhaled loudly through his nose and turned to stare out of the window. The Scotland Yard man nudged the Cabinet Minister but provoked no response. The Minister continued to stare at the nape of the Whitehall spokesman's neck. For a few moments nobody spoke, and there was a minor flutter at the door beside me when Miss Harley of Photo-Copying arrived late. We all ignored her, of course.

'At three o'clock this morning,' continued the man who had been speaking – his name was Bidley and he had a long career in the Civil Service although he never amounted to much – 'in a joint operation undertaken by the Special Branch and the CID, George Blake was apprehended and taken into custody.'

There was a stunned silence in the room. None of us knew who on earth this George Blake was supposed to be. Raymond Gray broke the ice, typically drawing attention to himself by exclaiming loudly, 'Oh, the bastard!' and bringing his hand down sharply on the back of one of the bentwood chairs which fell into bits.

'As I am sure you are all aware,' went on Bidley eventually, 'George Blake is the Soviet agent we have been after for some time.' The room was filled with murmurs of 'Oh yes,' and 'Blake, eh?' and 'Good show.' I nodded my head vigorously, not wishing to appear the odd man out.

'Blake has been remanded in custody, but in a preliminary de-briefing he has put the finger on a high-ranking MI6 Section Officer who he claims to be a long-term deep-penetration Soviet double agent. A mole.'

Immediately the attitudes of those present polarized. The junior staff turned to one another, expressing their concern and apprehension. The high-ranking MI6 Section Officers in the room struck poses of great dignity and trustworthiness, suddenly looking reassuringly British. The civil servants and the Cabinet Ministers caught one another's eyes, and the Scotland Yard man grinned like a lynx, his beady eyes darting about to take in the reactions of the senior Department officials.

Bidley clearly relished the effects of his words. 'I believe,' he went on, 'that you all appreciate the gravity of the situation. For the time being, that is all the information that is available.'

'Not quite all the information,' said another voice, and Bidley looked suddenly put out at being shunted from the centre of the stage. The other speaker was one of his Civil Service colleagues, Claude Taylor, and a moment before he spoke I had noticed the Cabinet Minister touch him lightly on the arm and nod. The Scotland Yard man, apparently unsettled at the prospect of a revelation he had not expected and which would deprive him of the satisfactory process of detection, looked grumpy. Elsdon, still staring out of the window, smiled.

'The name of the high-ranking MI6 official implicated by Blake is known to us,' pronounced Taylor, fixing all those present with a steely eye, which took some time. 'Information which has been turned up in our records confirms his identity. It is my sad duty to inform you that the KGB agent who has been among us for many years is a man for whom we have all had at times great respect. His name is Kim Philby.'

The news was received in utter silence. Not even Raymond Gray was prepared to chance any display of reaction under the fierce gaze of the Cabinet Minister, his three civil servants, the man from Scotland Yard and a roomful of extremely edgy Section staff. We all knew that Philby had been the subject of some speculation in the mid-fifties, but such doubts about his loyalty to the Crown as there were had only come from the CIA, whose motives in stirring up trouble in the Department were clear to everyone – especially after the Suez mishap – and Philby's reputation had been rapidly and completely laundered by the Prime Minister himself in the House of Commons. With this news of Philby's fall from grace, we all realized that none of us in that room could now consider ourselves or each other to be above the gravest suspicion. A particularly shifty attempt at casual confidence now seemed to afflict those junior staff members who had in the past linked the destiny of their careers with the great Philby, had cultivated a relationship with him during his early meteoric rise, had defended his name against the taunts of his persecutors, and had kept in touch with him during his years in the wilderness, hoping for favours on his triumphant palm-strewn return. Least convincing of all their performances was that of Raymond Gray.

'That, ladies and gentlemen,' said the third civil servant, who had not so far spoken, 'concludes the meeting. I'm sure that you will all absorb and react to this information in what you consider to be your own appropriate ways. Thank you.'

Others were to tell me that this man was Head of Internal Security at the Admiralty, and understandably rather a bitter type. The threat contained in his statement, which I confess I did not spot at the time, was said to be that if the Department did not set its house in order, the Admiralty would take over the running of MI6 for an indefinite period. That prospect filled us all with horror, not least myself, who knew only too well that organization's evangelical dedication to the introduction of A4 stationery, which would have thrown our own perfectly adequate foolscap filing system into – and I am not overstating my case, for Agnes was to agree with me – chaos.

The Scotland Yard man took a pace forward. 'Before you all go,' he began, but the Cabinet Minister coughed quietly and shook his head, so we all left.

Later on it turned out that the Scotland Yard man had been there by mistake. Wires had got crossed, and he had nothing at all to do with the Philby business. He was only there to winkle out any information there might be about a hired Ford Anglia, paid for by a Section warrant, recently discovered in a Harpenden pub car park where it had been dumped in 1956.

That evening most of the staff were to meet again in the canteen at Stockwell for Dennis Dobbs' retirement party. After many years of ill-health and frankly bad luck, Dobbs had been awarded a Section pension, and we were gathered to give him a good send-off. Memories of the Balham meeting cast an uneasy pall over the party, and the atmosphere was not helped by the absence of Dobbs himself, electrocuted that afternoon while trying out an electric carving-knife sent to him as a retirement present by an anonymous well-wisher. The hospital said his condition was 'comfortable', but the mood of the celebration was gloomy.

There was a great deal of drink, of course, and some of the Aunties had done sterling work providing mushroom vol-au-vents, small pieces of moist toast smeared with mashed sardine, lumps of cheddar and pineapple on toothpicks, anchovies and olive halves on Ritz crackers, bowls of crisps and nuts, and all the usual fare. Elsie, flat-mate and assistant to Agnes, had come up with four platefuls of what she described as 'something of an experiment really', with a self-effacing giggle. These confections consisted of a morsel of sausage dipped in Parmesan cheese, a maraschino cherry and a marshmallow, all skewered on a Twiglet. Several people tried one.

Although it was hardly seasonal, there were crackers. I pulled mine with Agnes, and in an attempt to jolly along the proceedings I donned the orange tissue crown with silver paper crescent. The trinket contained in the cardboard tube was a key-ring from which dangled rather a lurid yellow plastic skull. Agnes took a pull at her tumbler of punch and urged me to read the motto. Chuckling with the *bonhomie* I felt it my duty to assume, I unrolled the slip of paper and read the single word printed there. It said, 'Beware.'

It was later discovered that young Gosset of M Section had got at the crackers. His idea of a joke was to replace the authentic mottoes with sinister messages, but nobody found it a very amusing prank; Raymond Gray went very pale and had to sit down when he read 'The game is up' in his, and after the perpetrator was unmasked Gray became very annoyed, and according to Section folk-lore never spoke to Gosset again.

At one point during the evening I heard a squeal from the corner where Agnes was dispensing her fruit punch. A girl pushed her way through the crush in my direction, and with surprise I recognized her as Carol Moon, the young Auntie who had wept on my shoulder some five or six years before. I had not seen her since, and it had been my belief that she was no longer employed by the Department.

'Hello,' I said, as she brushed past. The girl turned to me and I saw that she was furious.

'The trouble with this bloody Department is that there's too many bull-dykes.' She stormed off to the other end of the room and struck up an animated conversation with a male colleague. I watched them for a few moments. Although he was not anyone I worked with regularly, there was something tantalizingly familiar about the man's face. I knew him from somewhere, yet I simply couldn't put a name to him, nor could I remember where or when we had been in contact. It didn't matter of course, as I told myself. After all, one fat young man looks very like another.

However, Carol Moon's angry remark had set me pondering. In view of Philby's exposure earlier that day, I began to worry that Section paranoia was reaching a dangerous level. I was beginning to feel it in myself, and there was something in what she had said that puzzled and worried me.

I sought out Raymond Gray. After some time I found him, fully recovered from the shock of his cracker motto, in a nook below the Burger Bar comforting Elsie who was, as usual, in a state. Taking him to one side I spoke to him seriously.

'Gray, at a time when we are all trying to cope with the concept of "moles" and "corkscrews" and "nutcrackers" I think it only fair that your Jargon Division should act responsibly and cut down on introducing new terminology without complete Section clearance.'

Gray didn't know what I was on about, but I soon told him.

'A colleague has recently used a term I have not yet been memo-ed on. What exactly is the status or function of a bull-dyke?'

Unexpectedly Gray laughed, then turned away to cope with a new burst of sobbing from Elsie. He dismissed me in the cavalier fashion I had worked so hard not to resent. 'I believe,' he smiled, 'a bull-dyke is something you'll find in Records.'

Leaving Gray, who was obviously not prepared to give a straightforward response to my query, I crossed the room to the corner where Agnes, ladle in hand, was manning the punch bowl. I asked her, as Head of Records, if she knew what a bull-dyke was. Her reaction was swift and forceful, and it was to take two visits to the dry cleaners before the stains on my waist-coat were completely removed.

The incident cheered up the party for a moment, but on the whole the evening was glum. As far as I could tell, no one there mentioned Philby at all, rattled as they were by the revelation at the safe-house in Balham. I understood their reticence, although I had not been so affected by the disclosures as they were. I alone had already known the identity of the traitor unmasked by Blake. Two days earlier Bill Elsdon had told me.

Ten

Arriving at the office next morning, I was surprised to learn that Bill Elsdon had retired. He was known to be over sixty-five, but it was a tradition in the Department that we did not adhere blindly to the Civil Service rule of retirement by age. Retirement by choice, as in the church, had always been our standard practice – George Bungay of Office Furniture Deployment and later Chief of Satellite Remote Intelligence Gathering carried on well into his eighties – but Elsdon had elected retirement with no warning to his colleagues, and that very evening had left the country for the Mediterranean bungalow of his dreams. He was to be sadly missed, not least by myself, and I confess that a lump came to my throat as I read his final farewell memo on my desk. As a postscript, he added that he would be obliged if I would have an interview that afternoon with a man called Skardon.

This Skardon turned out to be a very nosey type. I brought our interview to a swift conclusion by assuring him that there were no vacancies in W Sector at present, and recommended him to look for a post as a Nose-wiper.* He left my office reluctantly and apparently confused.

What with the unmasking of Philby and Elsdon's retirement, the whole staff of MSI Section were in a bit of a

* Nose-wipers are low-security personnel who accompany home-based agents on their occasional trips abroad to look after their tickets, hotel bookings, and to see that they eat properly, the name having been introduced in 1961 in preference to Raymond Gray's original suggestion.

flutter for a while. Raymond Gray was livid when the order came down from the civil servant Claude Taylor that all Department personnel were to hand over their private address books for scrutiny. I handed mine in for inspection at the same time as Gray, and noticed that he was offering up rather a new and cheap-looking book with very few entries as far as I could see.

After Elsdon's disappearance from the scene, Helen and I would occasionally speculate, over a spot of late-night toasted cheese, on the possibility of my filling his shoes. The thought of becoming S excited me greatly, although I was careful never to show it; and Helen surprisingly seemed more than happy at the prospect, perfectly content to accommodate the irregular hours and my frequent absences from home that the new and better paid job would entail. We even went so far as to write off to several estate agents for details of properties in Penge, a pleasant residential area after which we had both frequently hankered.

As it was, my hopes of promotion were rapidly dashed. Elsdon's successor was not to be myself, nor was it to be Raymond Gray, whose Eastern Medium Sized Islands had turned out over the years to be so much more dramatic, challenging and flashy than my own operations in the West. Gray had dined out on his Formosa stories long after that island had been re-assigned to SEA Section. Disappointed as I was upon hearing that I could forget promotion and Penge, the thought that Gray was not to become my superior came as some sort of relief.

Elsdon's successor was to be the civil servant Claude Taylor. In fact Taylor was one of those who had spoken at the Balham meeting. For a few days after his appointment the Department SRBs were devoted to the pooling of information on the man who was to be our new S. Late of the Household Cavalry and now making his way through the hierarchy of espionage, Taylor was generally reckoned to be a decent type, and I for one did not resent his new promotion, although he was a good eight and three-quarter years younger than myself. He soon began to be seen around Section HQ, popping in unexpectedly to this office or that just to make himself known to the staff. His nickname, as we were later to discover, was 'Tinker'.

I was puzzled by Elsdon's precipitate retirement because I knew that he was in the middle of handling something big. It was unlike S to give up a case before all the t's and i's had been crossed and dotted, and yet he had upped sticks and gone before the fragments of the Philby bombshell had been collected, collated and filed. I knew that Elsdon had some special interest in the Philby case as he had called me about it two days before the Balham meeting.

I had been working late. It was almost quarter to six, and my memo on the deplorable state of Sector personnel's footwear shine had nearly reached its final draft when the telephone rang.

'Geoffrey dear,' said Elsdon's voice with disarming intimacy, and slurred with emotion, 'I require the tiniest favour, and I trust that it is within your gift to grant me this small boon. I prostrate myself, salaam salaam.'

'Are you speaking in code?' I inquired cagily.

'Geoffrey, the manure is about to strike the air-conditioning apparatus.'

'Hang on while I get the code-book.'

'Alsop, I am trying to speak plainly. They have dug up a mole in our Department.'

'A mole? In the Department? A Communist Party recruiting cell?'

'No, that's a Hoover. A mole is a deep-penetration long-term Soviet agent. The Corkscrews have dug up a mole.'

'Lummee!' I exclaimed. 'Who is it?'

'Philby. Bloody Philby!'

'Oh. Well that's a bit of a shock.'

'Not to me,' said Elsdon icily. 'As a matter of fact that's why I'm calling you. I've been building up quite a case against our Kim for some time. If we can add it to the information already in the hands of the Corkscrews, they'll be able to sink him without trace. I want you to get them that information, Geoffrey.'

'Won't they find it on his Department file?'

'No, actually,' said Elsdon, and I was forced to admire the casual way in which he was imparting this shattering news. 'No, I've been keeping it somewhere safe. I'd like you to pick it up this evening and just sort of pop it into Philby's file.'

'Will do,' I replied eagerly, feeling admittedly a little stimulated at being brought so close to the heart of things.

'Not a word to a soul,' cautioned Elsdon.

'Of course not. Where is this information on Philby?'

'Oh it's in my personal file as a matter of fact, an unattributed dossier code-marked "Agent Icarus". I'd just like you to swap it over to Philby's file where it belongs.'

For a moment I could not speak, aghast at the audacity of my superior. Fancy storing explosive material like this Icarus dossier in your own personal file. If an A-rated Security sweep had landed Elsdon's file in the hands of the Nutcrackers, they might well have leapt to the conclusion that agent Icarus was Elsdon himself.

'Yes, of course,' I said, pleased with the steely ring of efficiency in my voice, 'I shall do it first thing in the morning.'

'No, do it tonight, please, Geoffrey,' said Elsdon, 'please, tonight.'

'Records will be closed by now.'

'No. At five-thirty Agnes generally still has one-third of a bottle to go. She'll still be there and the door will be open. Go and check if you like.'

'I believe you, S. Good heavens, if I can't trust you, who can I trust?' I said, and I meant it.

'Do you mean it, Geoffrey? Oh, God bless you, Geoffrey. Do it now.'

'I'll do it now,' I said, '. . . Bill.'

Elsdon sneezed or something, then hung up without another word. Resolving to complete the final draft of my memo the following morning, I locked up the office and slipped along the corridor to Records. There was no clear plan in my mind how to retrieve the Icarus dossier from its hiding place and insert it into Philby's personal file without exciting the curiosity of Agnes, but I have never been lacking in resourcefulness – as my handling of the inter-Section Whist Club dispute had clearly shown – and I resolved to play it by ear. Pushing the door ajar and peering into the gloom, I was pleased to discover that luck was on my side. Agnes – her bottle now empty – lay snoring loudly, sprawled among stacked sheaves of Transport Requisition Dockets dating back to 1953.

Softly, I closed the door behind me. Moving with more caution than was strictly speaking necessary, it did not take me many moments to locate Elsdon's file in the heap between the two wooden filing cabinets where I knew I would find it.

The Icarus file was a simple manilla folder containing two foolscap sheets of flimsy paper. The information – in double-spaced typing rather sloppily punctuated and corrected in ink, which put the date of its writing to my mind as sometime in early 1950 when the Department Tipp-Ex correcting fluid allocation had gone haywire – consisted mainly of a list of dates and events, roughly cross-referenced and annotated here and there by hand. It was dynamite. Obviously I cannot reveal here the full contents of those pages, but I can report that the agent Icarus, recruited by Comintern some time in the early 1930s, had enjoyed a long and fruitful career within the Department working for the Russian Intelligence services. Rising rapidly to a succession of senior posts within MI6, he had been involved in several covert operations on behalf of his Soviet masters, not least of which was the part he could clearly be seen to have played – according to a later, hand-written addendum – in the defection of Burgess and Maclean. Rapidly scanning and assimilating this white-hot information, I slipped Elsdon's personal record back into the heap and carried the Icarus file towards the dim recesses of the room where I knew I would locate Philby's dossier within the foothills of the mountain range of piled documents that rose from the linoleum towards the 40-watt glow in the green enamel lampshade that hung high above them and was even in daylight the only light that fell upon them and the overstuffed filing cabinets and sagging shelves and the solid walls of paper that filled the window space from sill to pelmet. I had spent many hours in the past finding my way around Records when a request for this or that item had been met with a harrassed 'Find it yourself', and I now moved with practised ease through the familiar gloom which had in the course of time taken such a toll of Agnes' eyesight.

Philby's record was where I expected it to be. Luckily it was one of the files in the heap with its spine outward and so was comparatively easy to locate. As I slipped it from its resting place, the papers above it shifted slightly and several large envelopes and folders tied with green garden twine slid gently from the peak and slithered down into a dark trough where they landed with a clinking sound among a nest of empty bottles, and a voice behind me whispered, 'What are you doing?'

I called out in surprise and whirled around to find Elsie peeping fearfully at me over a hillock of maps rolled up in cardboard tubes. She held a paper cup of coffee in one hand. She must have been over to the canteen to fetch it for Agnes. My cry startled her and she spilt some of the coffee.

'It's only me,' she said.

'Yes, well,' I replied, hoping to reassure her, 'it's only me, too.'

'What are you doing?'

'Nothing much,' I said in an offhand way, but I could see from her face she wasn't satisfied by this reply.

'Actually,' I went on casually, 'I just popped in to check something and as Agnes was asleep I just came over here and checked it. Well, I've checked it now. Yes,' – and here I wagged the Icarus file at her – 'it's been checked all right. So now I'm putting it back in the file. There we are, it's back in the file it came out of. See? There it is, back in the right file and checked. So that's fine, isn't it?'

I shoved the Philby record, now containing the report on agent Icarus, back in its place and brushed the dust from the front of my suit. Elsie watched without speaking as I left. I did think of asking her not to bother Agnes by mentioning my visit, but I knew she would tell her anyway, and in any case I was pretty sure Agnes would soon forget she'd been told. I had also been very careful not to let Elsie see that it was Philby's dossier I was holding, so there would be no way of their finding out what I had been up to.

After leaving for home, I telephoned Bill Elsdon from the call-box across the street. When he answered, I simply said, 'Mission accomplished,' and hung up straight away. A moment later, I dialled his number again, and heard him pick up the receiver almost at once.

'Yes?' he said sharply.

'Hello. That was Geoffrey Alsop calling you just then. Thought I'd better let you know in case you were wondering.'

'Who's that?'

'It's me again.'

Elsdon, always a stickler for security, hung up very quickly.

When I came out of the call-box I looked across at headquarters. A figure stood looking out of one of the windows. It might have been Elsie, but I couldn't tell as the light was behind her. To be on the safe side I did a bit of shrugging and so forth.

At home I was surprised to find Raymond Gray just leaving. He said he had popped round to see me, but had just given up and been about to go. He assured me that

Helen had entertained him splendidly, and said how lucky I was to have such a wife, and Helen blushed and told him to shut up in a jokey sort of way. I asked him why he had wanted to see me, and he explained that he only wanted to let me know that he had visited Dennis Dobbs that afternoon to see how he was getting on, and had found him in rather a grouchy mood following a scorpion bite. Poor old Dobbs, we agreed, and then Gray went.

Later that night I had an unfortunate scene with Helen. On going to bed I noticed that there were clean sheets on the bed for the second time in two days. Helen explained that she had rolled over on to a praline which had fallen from the dairy assortment she had been eating in bed that morning and made a bit of a mess. I'm afraid I spoke rather sharply on the matter and Helen had a bit of a weep. I hate to see a woman cry, especially Helen, and the incident made me realize how edgy I was becoming, caught up as I was in events beyond my control and even my ken, and which I must not divulge even to my wife. I apologized and patted her here and there, managing to soothe her by saying that of course I understood how much her little contributions to the housekeeping meant to her, but not to feel obliged to run up laundry bills for the sake of nothing more than a stained sheet or two.

Shortly afterwards Philby, who had disappeared from Beirut, turned up in Moscow. On 1 June of that year – 1963 – he was officially identified as the Third Man, which came as no surprise to me.

Eleven

Since the Balham revelations of the previous year we had all been aware that it was only a matter of time before Philby made a run for it. When that speculation became a reality, most of us reacted coolly with a wise nod of the head and as often as not some sage remark about 'chickens coming home to roost', or 'he who sups with the devil', or – surprisingly in little Elsie's case – 'let him first cast out the mote that is in his own eye', which I must confess went right over my head. Raymond Gray for once said nothing, but went around for days whistling the Harry Lime theme.

Most of us felt that this was the end of the affair. Section work returned to the sane and simple pace to which we were accustomed and indeed in most cases devoted. I was particularly pleased to be able to return to the unexciting yet rewarding Sector work which I had temporarily been forced to neglect, and was especially happy with the outcome of our operation in Newfoundland – masterminded by myself – which revealed that part of a certain batch of canned salmon destined for a warehouse in Nine Elms had found its way into the hold of a Soviet submarine prowling the North Atlantic coast of Canada. I am not a vindictive man, but I confess I felt a certain glow of satisfaction when we heard shortly afterwards that all tins in that particular consignment which had reached the UK had been condemned by the Department of Public Health and Hygiene, and I could hardly resist a smile as I congratulated myself on not being one of the unfortunate submariners who had consumed the suspect salmon in the cramped quarters of their vessel as it cruised deep below the polar ice-cap.

Things returned to normal. Claude Taylor settled in behind what had been Elsdon's desk with ease and efficiency, although there were those who claimed to miss Bill Elsdon's flamboyance and flair. Taylor nevertheless brought a sense of stability to MSI headquarters, and our working days took on the sort of safe and comfortable sense of routine which I cherished. The only thorn I was aware of in my flesh was Dennis Dobbs – retired of course – who took to phoning me frequently at all hours of the night with some paranoid theory that the Department was trying to do away with him. In spite of my sleepy reassurances, he persisted in his conviction and from time to time his calls made my life in the bedroom very difficult indeed. It was hard to take his wild accusations seriously, and I put his peculiar state of mind down to the effects of the antimony poisoning he had recently suffered.

The Department pottered on at its familiar pace for several weeks, then once again a bombshell fell metaphorically into our laps. A handful of senior Section officers were abruptly called upon to attend a meeting at four o'clock in the afternoon of a dismal Wednesday in September. It is only now, after public disclosures made in 1979, that I can reveal the matter of that briefing.

The tea-time meeting was to take place at Taylor's house. Not unnaturally – having no idea at the time of what was in the wind – I assumed that he was calling some of his more responsible subordinates over for tea in order to meet them on a social footing and thus get to know them better. Accordingly I brought with me – in addition to my briefcase and overcoat – a Madeira cake in a brown paper bag to present to Mrs Taylor by way of a thank you for her anticipated hospitality.

The Taylors lived in a large and gracious property – built quite recently, but Georgian in style – off a long sweeping avenue of copper beeches in Virginia Water. I was last to arrive, having taken the wrong exit at one of the roundabouts on the A4 and having sped several miles on the A30 towards Basingstoke before realizing my navigational error. Taylor showed me swiftly into the lounge where the others were waiting; Raymond Gray, Agnes, Lawson the Department Field Co-ordinator, and Spiers who had taken over as Assistant Head of MSI replacing Clive Black, now in Beirut. The room was large and airy but the company were gathered in one corner, perched on upholstered but business-like upright chairs. A young Nursemaid called Ted Lynn with a reputation for wildness but a useful man in a tight spot stood in front of the french windows with his back to the room.

Taylor got down to brass tacks right away. As there were no refreshments in evidence I could see that this was not to be a social gathering, and thought it best to conceal the Madeira cake I had brought by pushing it under the chair I was on with the back of my heel.

The subject of the briefing was no less a person than Sir Anthony Blunt. His Communist associations had been known to MI5 for many years, and his name had cropped up from time to time in both official and semi-official rumours. Following the defection of Burgess and Maclean in 1951, he had been questioned by MI5, but they were unable to establish a connection. He had been interrogated again in 1952 and in '53, then more or less annually for the next ten years. In 1956 he had been knighted by Her Majesty the Queen, and in 1958 awarded the French Légion d'honneur. Still he did not crack. Finally, as Taylor explained, the disappearance of Philby had either thrown up new evidence or removed the necessity for Blunt's continued silence, and the MI5 boys had winkled out a confession at last.

'Well good for them,' exclaimed Raymond Gray, all inter-Departmental jealousy apparently put aside.

'How deep was he?' asked Spiers, the Assistant Head.

'Pretty deep,' said Taylor. 'Seemingly Blunt helped arrange

the escape route for Maclean, then Philby got him to put him back in touch with the Russians in 1954 or '55 when the heat was on.'

'My God, Fleet Street are going to have a field day with this one,' growled Agnes, eyeing a reproduction Queen Anne cocktail cabinet in the alcove behind Taylor.

'I'm afraid not,' said Taylor, 'because they're not going to know about it. There seems a great deal more to this business than even we are aware of. Even MI5. Remember our masters in Whitehall have always been adamant that under no circumstances whatsoever should any of those involved in this case stand public trial. That is why, as you will recall, they had all manner of pink fits when it was rumoured in the press that Burgess and Maclean were planning to return to this country in 1962. They would have had to have been arrested. They would have had to have stood trial. And God knows what unholy can of worms we would have had to have allowed to have been opened.'

'I don't quite understand,' I chipped in. 'Is there some sort of problem over this Blunt character?'

'Of course there's a bloody problem,' said Taylor really quite sharply. 'The man refuses to defect.'

There was a pause as his words sunk in.

'He won't go?' said Spiers at length, looking aghast.

'He won't go, and Whitehall won't let him stand trial.' Taylor stood up and walked across the room and stared out of the french windows. Ted Lynn opened the window in front of him to let him out but Taylor glared at him so he shut it again.

'So what happens to him?' asked Spiers. Taylor made a noise like a bark and spun round towards us.

'What do you think happens?'

Raymond Gray moved uneasily in his chair, and as no one else seemed prepared to offer any suggestions I felt obliged to speak.

'Termination, I suppose.'

Taylor stamped his foot. 'You can't put the Keeper of the Queen's bloody Pictures on a bloody hit-list.'

'Then what happens?' asked Spiers again.

'I'll tell you what happens. Nothing. Would you believe Whitehall have granted him immunity?'

It took some moments for the implications of these words to sink in. At least, it did in my case. I was just opening my mouth to speak, getting in before Gray for once, when the door behind us opened and our host's wife bustled in. She was a long thin grey woman with a face like a whippet.

'Tinker, I'm taking the dogs over to Marjorie's for a run,' she announced breezily. 'I'll be back in half an hour.'

'Yes, dear.'

'And you won't forget we've got the Major and his brood descending on us for drinkies at five-thirty.'

'No, dear.'

'No, of course you won't. And when I get back I expect you to have got rid of all these beastly men. Oh hello, Raymond. You've all got to be off by five-fifteen to give Mrs Bright time to clear up and air the room.'

'Yes, dear.'

'Goodness, what long faces. You men take everything so seriously.'

She shut her eyes tight and smiled briefly and was gone.

'Piss off, dear,' said Agnes under her breath, but I think Taylor heard her.

Our Chief spent the final twenty minutes of the meeting impressing upon us the fact that what we had been told was to be kept an absolute secret. In a way there was no reason to have told us anything, but as Taylor said, we would hear the rumour soon enough and it was better that we be told the full official story and then sit on it. Blunt, the confessed Communist agent, was to be allowed to pursue his distinguished career protected from the attentions of the law.

By five fourteen I was on the road again – the A320 – and heading for home. As I drove along I pieced together all that I knew about the case, and at last it seemed that all the bits were going to fit.

In 1945 Philby was Head of Russian Section in the Department, Maclean was Secretary of the Anglo-American Committee on Atomic Weapons in Washington, the outrageous Burgess was making contact with the less respectable and thus potentially blackmailable elements in the political and social hierarchy, and Blunt was carving himself a secure academic niche within the Establishment. Moscow must have been rubbing its hands with glee. The unholy quartet must have seemed safe as houses. Nothing appeared capable of harming them. In 1945 a minor Soviet diplomat named Volkov turned up at the British Consulate in Istanbul, offering to reveal the names of three Russian agents working within MI6, in exchange for political asylum. MI6 were delighted at the prospect, and sent out their Senior Officer in Russian Sector, Kim Philby. By the time he arrived in Istanbul Volkov had disappeared and was never seen again, unless – as some believe – the completely bandaged figure bundled into a Russian airliner which had made an unscheduled stop at Istanbul airport was the luckless diplomat.

It is painful to admit that we have the Americans to thank for breaking up our nest of moles. In 1949 Philby took up the post of First Secretary to the British Embassy in Washington. There he aroused the suspicions of the CIA, and the KGB were obliged to place him on the 'temporarily inactive' list.

In 1951 suspicion fell upon Maclean, and it was arranged to bring him in for surprise interrogation on Monday 28 May. Philby, the Third Man, got wind of this in Washington and warned Maclean just in time, and alerted Burgess who then enlisted Blunt's help in organizing Maclean's immediate escape, and on 25 May Burgess and Maclean defected to Moscow.

Curiously enough it has since been established that the original plan had been for Maclean alone to leave the country. It must have been a last minute decision by Burgess to accompany him, and it proved a rash move. Never a master of the low profile, Burgess left a paper-chase a mile wide across the continent as they hurried towards Moscow. On the cross-channel ferry he insisted on spending the trip in the bar, where he and Maclean stood drinking beside two British journalists who were quite unaware of the identity of this pair of fellow travellers. On leaving the boat Burgess left behind in the cabin his suitcase containing a few items of underwear and a couple of London telephone directories to give it weight. Furthermore, because of his known association with Burgess, Philby was called in for questioning and even asked to resign – which he refused to do – and remained on the MI6 payroll until after his name was officially cleared by the Prime Minister in the House of Commons in 1955, when he was promptly dismissed.

At about this time Blunt put Philby in touch with Moscow again to arrange his ultimate defection, which did not become necessary until George Blake was arrested in 1962 and firmly put the finger on Philby who disappeared on 23 January of the following year. This brought us just about up to date with Blunt's subsequent confession and guarantee of immunity.

Pleased with my grasp of the flow of events and satisfied with its neatness, I was still turning the story over in my mind as I fell asleep beside Helen that night. I believe I was chuckling aloud at my dream of Burgess and Maclean and Philby ringing and ringing and hammering at the door of the Kremlin to be let in when I suddenly awoke to realize there was somebody at the front door. The time was after one in the morning.

I could see nothing through the bedroom window which was now stuck utterly fast. Dragging my dressing gown around me I hurried downstairs and opened the front door on the chain.

Four men stood on the doorstep.

Twelve

The four men in plain clothes identified themselves as members of the Special Branch. They asked if they could come in and I could see no way of preventing them.

They brought disturbing news. Apparently the Bomb Disposal Squad had been called out to Claude Taylor's house that evening. No information was at that time available on the incident, but it was believed that there were no casualties. As a routine procedure full-scale security sweeps had been ordered on the homes of all Senior Section Staff, which was why they were here. I was more than happy to allow them to search the premises for anything suspicious, and Helen – who had appeared in her night-dress at the top of the stairs, wide-awake – insisted on helping the four strapping young officers in their investigations under the beds and in dark corners. At about three o'clock she made them all some cocoa before seeing them off after their fruitless search.

That night I did not sleep well. In the morning I was off early to Section headquarters, relieved in a way to see one of the Special Branch men still outside in his car apparently keeping an eye on the house. Arriving at my office I discovered on the desk a Most Urgent memo requesting all senior personnel to report to Taylor as soon as they arrived. I hurried down to his room and was delighted to find him all in one piece at his desk. Standing beside him was a Senior Bomb Disposal officer. Both had very stern faces. In front of them, on the blotter, in the soggy remains of its brown paper bag, lay my Madeira cake. Taking it in turns, they spoke to me rather fiercely after I had owned up.

Back in my own office I discovered a most puzzling thing. It was a cable from Clive Black in Beirut. I had not heard from him since his sudden posting there as Head of Hospitality which had left me stranded in Banbury. To tell the truth, I had not even known if Black was still with the Department as nobody ever spoke of him. His cable made no sense at all. It merely said 'CHECK BOOKS'.

I filed it and forgot about it. Later in the morning I took a call from Raymond Gray. He was only in the next office but occasionally he would use the telephone rather than get himself up and take the trouble of walking through the door. I knew he was about to twit me with regard to the Madeira cake and so prepared myself.

'Heard about the cake,' he began. 'Bad luck.'

He sounded most subdued, and I suspected he was up to something but I was happy to play him along.

'Thank you, Raymond. Is that all you called to say?'

'Actually no, it's about Dobbs.'

It had been a trying night and morning.

'Bloody Dobbs!' I exploded. 'I'm sorry, Raymond, you know I'm not one to swear, but that man is getting to be the limit. You know he's a loony. He is. Dobbs is a loony. Nearly every day now he's on at me about some half-baked paranoid plot. I really don't want to know about Dobbs and his imaginary problems. As far as I'm concerned, Dobbs is a pain in the bottom.'

'Dobbs is dead,' said Gray quietly. 'I knew he was a friend of yours, and thought you should be told.'

Feeling awful, I thanked Gray and hung up.

I heard the full story later on. Apparently the previous afternoon, while we had all been at our top-level meeting with Claude Taylor, Dobbs had arrived at Section headquarters in Stockwell and started making a fuss. He had forced his way into the building and demanded to see Taylor and on being told that S was not in his office had created a mighty fuss in the corridor, screaming 'blue murder' – those were literally his words – and throwing this and that around the place, even breaking a window and assaulting a female employee who had just arrived for work – Carol Moon as a matter of fact, who was still operating at Stockwell although I was never sure in what capacity, as we saw her so seldom – and on being restrained by the Security Staff had gone quite berserk. Struggling free and snatching up a staple gun, he had accused everyone in sight of trying to kill him and threatened anyone who dared to approach him that he would pin their ears to the clubs and societies notice board.

The police had eventually been summoned, and after a concerted rush by the constables and Section Security officers, Dobbs was disarmed and taken to the police station. The police insisted that certain witnesses should accompany them to give statements and four or five staff members agreed to go along, including Carol Moon and Terry Pope, our Senior Door-Keeper, who was driven away in a police van as soon as the officers had managed to unpin his left ear from the bottom of the squash ladder.

In the morning it was discovered that Dobbs had committed suicide while in police custody. We were all very upset that he should have ended like that, and some of us perhaps felt a twinge or two of guilt, but obviously he had been as mad as a hatter and there is a limit to what you can hold yourself responsible for. Dobbs had done away with himself by means of a massive self-administered injection of sodium pentothal. At least, we consoled ourselves, it would have been a peaceful end. The syringe was never found.

Nothing very exciting happened after that for the next fourteen years or so. The defection scandal was forgotten, although there was a minor flap in 1965 when we heard that Kim Philby – now in Moscow – had been awarded the Red Banner of Honour by the Soviet Union. After a heated discussion during one particular SRB I recall that it was mutually agreed that the Red Banner of Honour could be rated higher than a CBE although not as good as an OM.

Agnes was forced to retire as Head of Records at the age of eighty in 1968, by now quite blind. Elsie left with her and they both went to live in a cottage in Suffolk. Her retirement party was a sad affair, although Section personnel had clubbed together to buy her a set of bath towels as a retirement present.

The late sixties and early seventies were on the whole quiet times. The Falkland Islands operation occupied me a good deal and I was in frequent contact with my field-man, John Chappell. There was not, as far as I could see, any real security threat in that quarter, but Chappell was a conscientious and rather nervous type who sent me regular coded memoes which tended to fill my day.*

Inter-Departmental streamlining under the Taylor régime created one or two problems and led to a certain amount of time-wasting, and the inevitable introduction of metrication caused trouble in a dozen different ways. In 1977 a major Jargon Review was undertaken with the result that we said goodbye to the Nutcrackers and Corkscrews, both of these Divisions now being known collectively as the Toothpicks. It was in 1979 that things livened up considerably.

It had been asking far too much to expect the entire Secret Service to sit on the Blunt story for ever. After fifteen years the identity of the Fourth Man was pretty well common knowledge among the press, and when a positive rash of hints and revelations began to appear in print it eventually became clear to our political masters that it was impossible to keep the matter secret any longer. So it was that on Thursday 15 November of that year the Prime Minister, speaking from the floor of the House of Commons, revealed the name of Sir Anthony Blunt and his involvement with the defectors, thereby bringing down the self-righteous indig-

* See map at end of chapter.

nation and spiteful contempt of the British press and public upon the head of that distinguished – and by now quite harmless – academic. Her Majesty the Queen stripped him of his knighthood, though there were those who wondered why on earth she had given it to him in the first place, which she did in 1956 – the year of Burgess and Maclean's press conference in Moscow – at a time when he was under grave suspicion by the Department and regularly subject to interrogation. As a matter of fact, most of us had not realized that Honours could be taken back like that, and more than one of the senior Department members who had been less than discreet over the years in their attitude towards the confidentiality of the Blunt story began seriously to fear for their OBEs.

Not surprisingly, memories of the whole affair were very much in my mind as I pottered about at home that evening. Helen had gone out to visit a sick aunt, which she did regularly now at least once a week, and I was taking advantage of her absence to clear out some of the historical romances by Barbara Cartland which were overflowing from the lounge bookcase. Helen adored them and bought all the new paperbacks as soon as they appeared, devouring them with gusto. I swear she could read those books almost as fast as Miss Cartland could write them. She never threw any of them away, but every now and then I was allowed to skim off the surplus and store them in the attic.

I filled an old suitcase with the novels and went upstairs. Pulling down the folding ladder I mounted it to the attic. As I pulled the suitcase through the opening after me it jammed and I gave a tug. The worn leather handle broke and the case fell to the landing floor with a crash, bursting open and scattering books across the carpet. Looking down at the mess I was about to give a snort of aggravation when something caught my eye. On the battered lid of the suitcase were the initials RR, and I was suddenly reminded of my abortive cover-tracks mission to Banbury. And Clive Black.

And something else. Something else about Black. And books. His telegram.

I once straightened up very quickly in the kitchen under the open door of a wall-cupboard and caught my head a fearful crack that made my teeth buzz. I felt the same sensation now. Looking down at the picture below I had suddenly realized what Black's telegram had been about.

'CHECK BOOKS.'

I knew what it meant.

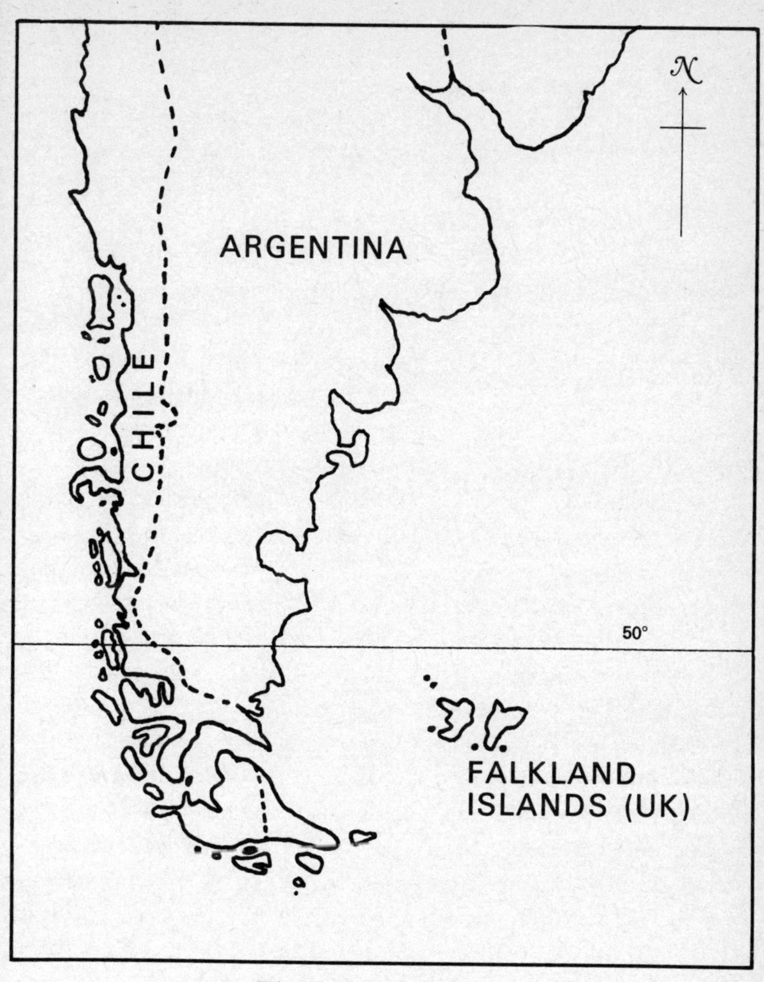

The Falkland Islands.

Thirteen

I halted the car halfway down the lane because the ruts and potholes I could see ahead were a menace to my exhaust. I pulled the parking brake up an extra notch on the ratchet to stop the car from rolling down the hill and stepped out into a hawthorn bush. No damage done, fortunately. Although the countryside round about was charming, this lane just off the main road – the A1071 – led down into a dark, untidy hollow. Agnes and Elsie's cottage was a low, grey, broken-backed structure with tiny windows and slanting walls, surrounded by heaps of abandoned building materials and rotting cardboard boxes that were piled against them; with a plume of oily smoke rising from the central chimney, and electric cables sagging between tilted poles and spars, it looked like a shipwreck.

Picking my way between the deep black puddles in the lane and across the scrubby unfenced garden patrolled by tattered bantams, I approached what I took to be the front door and knocked. It was eleven o'clock in the morning of the day after the evening when I had experienced that flash of insight into the meaning of Black's telegram at the top of the ladder to the loft. I had slept little that night, setting off bright and early hoping to reach Agnes' home just outside the delightful little village of Polstead before noon. I had made good time and was sure that Agnes would be at home, but as nobody had answered the door I knocked again more firmly and took a painful splinter in the knuckle.

Elsie appeared round the corner of the house and invited

me in through the other door which turned out to be the only one that opened. I had not seen Elsie for over ten years, and although she was looking undeniably older, it was plain that the country life agreed with her as she had put on a good bit of weight.

In the dim, low sitting-room sat Agnes. She was in a straight-backed rush-bottomed chair by the small window, a white stick at her side. What warmth there was in the sun fell across her face and shoulder. Elsie led me over to her and pushed me close.

'Agnes dear,' said Elsie, 'feel who's come to see you.'

The stained and clammy fingers reached up and pattered lightly across my nose, cheeks, mouth and spectacles.

'Oh, it's him,' grunted Agnes, reaching surely for the tumbler on the window-sill.

'How are you, Agnes?'

'Foul. How are you?'

'Sit down, Mr Alsop,' said Elsie, pushing an easy chair towards me, 'but be careful. One of the legs fell off. I'll make some tea.'

Elsie left and I perched myself cautiously on the edge of the seat, sucking my knuckle. Agnes and I sat in silence for some moments. I looked around the room at the furniture which somehow contrived to be both sparse and chaotic. There was an odd smell about the place, and I wondered if they had cats. Agnes picked her nose, and I reflected sadly how over the intervening years I had come to forget her little ways.

'We've seen some changes at Stockwell since you left,' I said.

'Bloody computers.' Agnes looked the same as ever although I realized with a shock that she must now be over ninety.

'They have their good points, Agnes.'

'No meat on the bone.'

'Perhaps not. Claude Taylor's still at the helm, you know.'

'Ha! At least old Bill Elsdon had balls.'

'Yes. Yes I suppose he did. Must have.'

A reflective pause followed. I knew that I must steer the conversation round to what I had a need to know.

'You heard about Blunt, I suppose?'

'Yes.' Agnes took a long swallow from the tumbler.

'What a crowd of jokers they all were, weren't they? Ha ha ha!'

'Were they?'

'Oh yes. Ha ha ha!' I rocked back and forth with counterfeit mirth, holding my sides to indicate how utterly amusing and unimportant I found the whole business, then, realizing that all this was lost on Agnes, I started slapping my thigh.

'Are you smacking something?'

'No, no, just laughing. Ha ha ha! You know – ha ha ha! – you know I think the most priceless thing was old Burgess on the boat, leaving that suitcase with the blinking telephone directories in it! Ha ha ha!'

'Where the hell's Elsie with that tea? And she'd better not skimp on the rum.'

'Oh that was funny that was. Ha ha ha. I don't suppose – ha ha, oh dear – I don't suppose you remember what happened to – ha – to the suitcase and the phone books? Eh? Ha ha. Where they went?'

'Elsie!' bellowed Agnes, then muttered, 'of course I know where they went.'

'Where?' I asked rather too quickly and I saw Agnes go on the alert.

'Why do you want to know?' she asked, something like a smile twisting her features.

'Oh, just idle curiosity,' I said dismissively and decided I should laugh a bit more.

'For God's sake, stop cackling.'

'I'm sorry but it just struck me as funny. You know where the suitcase is, but the computer hasn't the faintest idea. Ha ha!'

'Hasn't it?' Agnes was beginning to waver but still suspicious.

'So somebody told me.'

'Bloody computers,' said Agnes, draining her glass.

'You know though, don't you, Agnes? Of course you do. Not that it matters. I dare say it was filed away in some cellar at Field Ops. Or it went to the Grave-diggers.'

'Filed!' exclaimed Agnes. 'What do those cowboys know about filing?'

'Where did it go then?'

'Wouldn't you like to know.'

I sat for a moment studying her. She wasn't making it easy, but I thought she would come through in the end if I played my cards right.

'Agnes,' I murmured, 'where's the bottle?'

'Thought you'd never ask. It's over there, behind the commode.'

I crossed the room and fished the bottle out. 'This is Lucozade,' I said.

'I have an arrangement with the local grocer. He delivers it.'

As I filled her tumbler she groped for my lapel and pulled me close. 'Elsie doesn't suspect,' she hissed. Judging by the whisky fumes on her breath I found that statement hard to believe, but in a way I found it warming to know that this little deception – no doubt one among many others – kept their relationship alive.

Agnes took a generous gulp while I returned the Lucozade bottle to its place.

'So it wasn't filed?' I inquired.

'Filed?' Agnes almost choked. 'The bloody thing was raffled.'

'I'm sorry?'

'Raffled. Bill Elsdon had ordered the whole lot to be destroyed, but there was some big Home Office social do, and the organizers asked all the Departments to contribute something for their raffle. You know the sort of thing. A signed Prime Ministerial memo from the Whitehall office. A shoulder-holster from Special Branch. A tea-pot from the Nit-Pickers. Some bright spark in our section suggested Burgess's suitcase, so off it went.'

'Who suggested that?'

'Raymond Gray probably.'

'Not many people knew about this, I take it?'

'Not at the time. Elsdon found out later, of course. Tried to get it back from the winner, but they refused to part with it. Attached to it. Bizarre memento. Liked to show it off at cocktail parties.'

'Who actually did win it?' Casually.

'Dreadful beanpole of a woman. Deb-on-the-shelf-type, used to hang around the available Home Office chaps and the officers at Chelsea Barracks. Got herself invited to almost everything, she was so desperate to find a man. Monica Stirling-Wright.'

I was now so close, and yet I still had to proceed carefully if I was to arrive.

'Don't think I knew her,' I said conversationally. 'Monica Stirling-Wright? No. What – er – what became of her then?'

'Married Claude Taylor,' said Agnes as Elsie came in with the tea.

Fourteen

The three of us drank our tea in silence. It was indeed generously laced with rum, and after finishing hers Agnes fell off the chair. I helped to get her to the bedroom and then Elsie walked me to the car, not speaking till we got there.

'How has she been?' I inquired.

Elsie stared up into the low grey sky for some seconds before replying.

'She thinks a lot.'

'She always did. More than is good for her.'

'No, I said "thinks".'

'Ah yes.'

'Don't come here again,' she said suddenly.

'I had to, Elsie. I'm sorry if I upset her. I dare say Agnes never could stand the sight of me.'

'Oh no. Agnes is quite fond of you.' With that she turned away and staggered down the steep lane to the cottage which, wallowing in its dismal trough, was their home.

I thought about Burgess a great deal during the long drive back. I had recognized him from his newspaper photographs in 1951 as the man who had accosted me in the Stockwell Gents' a few months earlier. In the light of what I later learned about the man's character, that action was entirely in keeping with his social tendencies, yet for all his reputation for extrovert and ostentatious conduct, Burgess remained something of an enigma. He has been described as a spy and a traitor, but after years of listening to and assimilating rumour, conjecture and even highly-classified deep-penetration gossip I was still under the impression that he had never actually done anything.

Burgess had of course been involved with the Communists since his student days. He may well have been on the Soviet payroll throughout his career, and is thought to have recruited Blunt during his days as a Cambridge Apostle, but apart from that I have never heard of any activity undertaken by him that was likely to endanger national security. He never reached the positions of trust within the establishment or the Department enjoyed by Maclean, Philby and Blunt, although he did spend some years as producer of the radio programmes *The Week in Westminster* and *Can I Help You?*

There are those who argue that, as he never served in a post of importance, Burgess was useless to his masters in the Kremlin. This is not strictly speaking true, according to a rumour recently issued by Spiers. In 1949 and '50 for example, as a grade four officer in the junior branch of C Section he had access to highly sensitive British and American material including intelligence from Whitehall's JIC,* MI2, and the Supreme Command Allied Powers, Tokyo.† There is however no reason to suppose that any of this information reached the other side.

Why then did the Russians never make use of him? The answer seemed quite simple to me as I drove south-west through the early-afternoon drizzle. Quite frankly the man was a liability. His habits and dress were generally thought quite peculiar, his sexual tastes were not at all respectable, his drinking indiscriminate, and his general behaviour quite frequently grotesque. Chewing raw garlic, he was often heard at parties to announce that he was an agent of the KGB just to see the result of his disclosure on some fellow guest, and he would often leave wildly incriminating notes about his colleagues on some superior's desk, as a result of

* Joint Intelligence Committee.
† SCAPT.

which some twenty or so Department staff were actually dismissed over the years, and there was some bad feeling about that. None of these qualities would recommend him to the Russians for one of the delicate, low-key infiltration operations they so favour. Personally I wouldn't have employed him as a tea-boy, let alone a field-agent.

All this being so, I was at a loss to understand why he had fled. What had driven him to board the midnight cross-channel steamer *The Falaise* for the Southampton to St Malo trip on 25 May, 1951? What had he done to make him fly the land?

It was almost four o'clock when I reached Virginia Water. Taylor would not yet be home from the office, and I could only pray that his wife was in. She opened the door seconds after I had pressed the bell and heard the muffled chimes.

'Tinker's out,' she said and made as if to close the door again.

'Yes, I know,' I said quickly. 'He sent me here to pick something up. As a favour.'

'Oh! He might have let me know first. As a favour.'

'He sent his apologies.'

'Did he indeed?'

'And his love,' I improvised rapidly.

She looked at me quizzically then opened the door wide with a loud sigh. 'Well, I suppose,' she said, with great emphasis on the 'ose', 'you'd better come in. Wipe your feet and don't take any notice of Brutus,' she added, referring to a capable-looking boxer which had taken my hand gently in its mouth, friends for now. 'What exactly does he want?'

'As a matter of fact he's entertaining a working party of our American counterparts and he thought they'd be rather amused to see Guy Burgess' suitcase. And the phone books.'

'How curious. Well you'll have to wait in the kitchen while I go up and fetch them.'

She showed me into a charming kitchen decked out in

old pine with rows of glass jars on shelves and bunches of everlasting flowers hung up to dry in the window. I stepped through the doorway and immediately a Chihuahua shot across the floor like a rat and thrust its muzzle up my trouser leg.

'Sit down there,' commanded Monica Taylor, indicating a chintz-covered armchair in the corner on which a fat, unhealthy-looking spaniel grunted in its sleep. 'Chuck Mr Worthington on the floor, he won't mind. I see you've made friends with Snip.' The Chihuahua had snagged its teeth in my sock and couldn't have taken its head out of my trouser leg even if it wanted to.

While my hostess disappeared upstairs I shuffled across the kitchen floor, my hand still delicately gripped between the slimy jaws of Brutus. Gingerly I prodded Mr Worthington, then eased him carefully off the chair. He fell to the floor with a thud. I felt the grip of the Boxer's teeth grow firmer. Not daring to sit down now, I stood for a good ten minutes, the almost hairless Chihuahua wriggling against my ankle, the rheumy eyes of Brutus gazing up at me with distrust, and Mr Worthington lying on his back at my feet, belly rippling with every asthmatic snort and wheeze, pudgy legs in the air.

By the time Taylor's wife had returned with the case there were beads of sweat upon my brow and my spectacles were misty at the edges.

'Here you are,' she said, thrusting the suitcase into my free hand, 'and you can tell my dear husband that next time he sends his minions round on an errand he might let me know in advance. It's frightfully thoughtless, you know. In fact I've a good mind to call him now myself.'

'He's not in the office,' I said in a panic.

'You said he was.'

'Not in the office, no. He's entertaining the Americans somewhere else.'

'Where?'

'Leicester,' was my wild reply.

'He's in Leicester?'

'Not really Leicester. That's a code name for another place. Another place in London that isn't his office. And hasn't got a telephone.'

Brutus growled thickly. Monica Taylor shrugged and said, 'Oh such silly games,' but she seemed to accept my story. 'Well run along, I've got to go and feed the retrievers.'

I thanked her and made my way awkwardly towards the still-open front door. Halfway across the stone floor I stopped. I had never seen one before, but some absurdly calm analytical part of my brain told me that the muscular black beast with hackles raised that stood glaring at me from the doorway was a Doberman Pinscher. I groaned aloud, something I almost never do. Behind me Mrs Taylor exclaimed, 'Oh you bad boy, you've got out again.'

'Bad boy,' I repeated with what I hoped was authority. The animal displayed his teeth in a purposeful snarl.

'We haven't had him long,' said Mrs Taylor, joining me with a broom in her hands. 'We didn't have him as a pup, only got him six months ago in fact, and within a week he'd killed three of our dogs and we had to buy some more.'

'Can I get past him?'

'Oh probably. He's a magnificent specimen, isn't he?'

'Magnificent,' I agreed, trying to seem casual as I believe dogs are able to smell fear. 'Er . . . what's he called?'

'Smiley,' she replied, and at the sound of his name the Doberman covered the ground between us in a single bound and launched himself snarling towards me.

Brutus, God bless him, released my hand and hurled himself at the black dog's throat. They collided in mid-air with a tremendous thump and fell sprawling to the floor. The terrified Chihuahua scrabbled madly and disappeared completely up my trousers. The two big dogs, locked together in combat, whipped and bucked and whirled about while Mrs Taylor beat at them with the broom.

'They're not used to strangers,' she shouted. I raced for the door, calling out as casually as I could, 'Well I'll be off then.'

'Where's Snip?' she cried.

'I think they're eating him,' I replied, and ran out to the car as she beat about the animals with her broom. 'Bad boys,' she was shouting, 'spit him out.'

At the end of the driveway, some distance from the house, I stopped the car and got out. Undoing my trousers I was able to deliver the Chihuahua from within and slip him into the undergrowth. Speeding back to London I reminded myself that I was now operating under very short-term cover. If my theory was right it would have to show results fast.

Back in my office I locked the door. It was late now and few Section staff were about. I sat looking at the suitcase on my desk for a while, then snapped open the locks and lifted the lid. Inside, nestling on a bed of underwear, were the two telephone directories, the books that I believed Black had been referring to in his enigmatic cable. I chose one at random. It was L to R.

One and a half hours later I shut the book. Nothing. I felt the beginnings of a headache lurking behind my eyes but I knew that finding what I was looking for would not be easy, particularly since I was not altogether sure what it was that I was hoping to find. Raising my eyes I met the bespectacled gaze of Trotsky staring out of the photograph on the opposite wall. I had felt like giving up, but now I wondered what he would have done in my position. He would probably have gone to Mexico. With a sigh I opened the second telephone directory and began again the painstaking search. This one was A to D.

After ten minutes I had it. Under the letter G of the name Angus was a faint but unmistakable pin-prick. The next tiny indentation was under the O of Ardington, the next under the I of Arkwright, the N of Arlington, the G of Ashgrove. On a spare sheet of Department-issue rough paper. I scribbled down each letter as I found it. G-O-I-N-G. Going. Then the T of Atkins and the O of Atmos (Air-Conditioning). By eight fifteen I had the whole message decoded, the message which began 'Going to Moscow with Maclean.'

Burgess must have been desperate when he did it. Desperate to have used so simple an open code. But it was all there.

Transcribed on to the sheet of paper before me was the message Burgess had left behind. It described in detail the route which he and Maclean were to take to Moscow. It named the places at which they were likely to be delayed and therefore easily picked up by our Security people. Burgess had wanted Maclean to be stopped, had gone with him to ensure that he followed the intended route, and left instructions as to where and when this could be arranged. Burgess had been working for us all along. He was a triple agent.

Now I understood why, when he was approached by his KGB contacts to get Maclean out of the country – because he was known to have two tickets for the St Malo boat that evening, having planned a Paris weekend with an American friend – Burgess had decided to accompany him all the way. From St Malo they went to Rennes by taxi – having missed the train – and then by rail to Paris. From Paris they took the night express to Berne, where they sat for several hours in the restaurant before going on to Zurich and then – two days later – by plane to Prague. From Prague they flew to Moscow. Their progress was as obvious and clumsy and slow as can be imagined, they could have been intercepted at any time and brought back. They never were, in spite of the coded message in the A to D telephone directory that Burgess left behind. And that was not all.

If he and Maclean were not stopped and retrieved before crossing the Russian frontier, the pin-prick code also spelled out instructions on how Burgess was to be contacted, extricated and brought home. These instructions were not acted upon. Burgess died in Moscow in 1963. His final communication had been in the hands of the Department since the day of the defection yet it had never been de-coded. It had never been filed. It had been raffled.

Somebody in the Department had suppressed the Burgess message.

Closing the phone directory I turned to my in-tray. Before leaving home for Suffolk that morning I had called Records on the telephone, in particular the streamlined Personal Data Profile Unit (PDPU) and requested certain dossiers to be delivered to my office. The bulky pile lay on the desk before me. Such quick delivery would never have been possible in Agnes' day. Opening the first file I was disappointed to find that the information was all recorded on a series of punched cards. It was the same with the others.

I laid the useless dossiers out on my desk and arranged them in order. I imagined lines between them, making connections, collating what I knew with the dates and times I was struggling to recall, building up a network of relationships in my mind between the seven manilla folders, developing hypotheses, testing them, discarding them, trying again.

I sat staring at the files for ages.

And then I knew.

And then I went to Rickmansworth.

Fifteen

Raymond Gray rose from the bunk. I put out a hand to steady myself as *Water Goblin* tilted in the water at the shifting of his weight.

'Sit down, Geoff, and have a drink.'

I eased myself on to a padded cushion in a corner of the cabin by the steps. Gray set two glasses on the little plywood table that stuck out from the wall and filled them both generously from the bottle of Glenfarclas. He handed me one glass, then lifted his own.

'*Prosit*,' he said.

'Cheers,' I replied.

'You know, Geoff, there's no reason for us not to be civilized about this.'

'I had not imagined it any other way,' I answered him with a steely glare, but he had turned away to arrange some cushions before sitting down on the bunk again. By the time he turned back towards me I had stopped glaring. The moment had passed.

He sat staring at me for a time and then very slowly he began to grin. That was too much.

'Aren't you ashamed, Gray?' I exclaimed.

'Aren't you?' he replied. 'We're all in the same dirty business.'

In the heat of the moment I couldn't come up with an answer to that one so I said, 'Huh!' with some vigour, tossing my head back and catching it rather painfully on a bolt sticking out of the panel behind me.

'Are you all right?' asked Gray infuriatingly.

'Yes I'm fine. And I know everything.'

'Tell me what you know,' said Gray, leaning back and hitching his legs up on the bunk. I told him what I had discovered. He stared up at the light as he listened.

'And,' I concluded, 'you are the Fifth Man. The one who blocked Burgess' lifeline, who prevented him from accomplishing his objective, who stopped him from coming home.'

Gray leant across and topped up his glass. Mine was still untouched.

'Very good, Geoff. Very good indeed. Who would have thought it?'

It was my turn to grin, but somehow I felt it come out wrong.

'You realize, of course,' Gray said earnestly, swinging his legs off the bunk and leaning forward, 'that now you know too much.'

'Yes.' Much to my annoyance the word emerged in a husky treble.

'So you might as well get your facts right,' he said with a smile.

'What do you mean?'

'Well, on the Burgess stuff you're spot on. Good work there, Geoff. However, where you are in error is in your assumption that I am the Fifth Man.'

'You must be.'

'I ain't.'

This took me back a bit. For a moment I wondered if I could just apologize and ask him to forget I had said anything, but that would be silly. In any case, it would be natural for him to deny my accusation at first. I decided to carry on pressing and keep him on the defensive, a lesson Elsdon had taught me very early on.

'All right,' I said, 'if you weren't, who was?'

'Clive Black, of course.'

'That's ridiculous.'

'Yes he was.'

'Was he?'

'Oh yes.'

'Oh.'

It was some moments before I spoke again.

'It can't have been Black. He was the one who put me on to the phone books in the first place.'

'But that was much later,' said Gray, filling his glass yet again. 'Drink up. Look I'm only telling you this as a favour because your rummaging has landed you in a bit of a spot and as a colleague of several years' standing I think it's only fair you should know the truth. Now you haven't much time left so let me fill you in very briefly.'

'Go on,' I said quietly, raising my glass for a sip and then thinking better of it.

'In 1951,' Gray began, 'Black was a class three junior in Luggage Ordnance. The suitcase left by Burgess on the boat was Department issue and naturally returned to Black's Division. For some time, however, Black had been a Soviet sleeper, and on the orders of his handler, who also worked within the Department, was directed to dispose of the item *toute suite*.'

'So he raffled it off?'

'No.'

'Oh, sorry.'

'No, somebody else put it into the raffle before Black could destroy it. However, the removal of the suitcase from Department jurisdiction effectively blocked the Burgess connection, so Black was satisfied.'

'And his handler?'

'Not satisfied very much. He ran Black for a few more years, small jobs, nothing too taxing, but he never trusted him again. Then in 1956, Black got utterly cold feet. Philby was under suspicion, Burgess and Maclean were about to give a press conference in Moscow, and he thought he ought to get himself clear. He wanted to confess. He chose you, Geoffrey, and I believe he fixed a meeting with you in Banbury. Unfortunately for him, his handler got wind of it and had him posted to Beirut before he could see you.'

'How do you know all this?'

'Our people are very thorough. We know for example that Black was sent to Beirut so that Philby – who was already working there as a journalist – could keep an eye on him. In 1964, of course, after Philby had run to Moscow, Black felt he could take a chance. That's when he sent you the telegram.'

'Why me?'

'Well, I suppose because he thought you were the only person in the Department square enough to be trusted.'

I took a sip of the whisky. It tasted wonderful. In spite of everything I felt flattered – proud even – to hear that Black had felt he could trust me. In a way this was a surprise as he and I had exchanged several quite stinging memoes during the summer of 1954 when Black – as Deputy Head of Section – had championed the cause of the Covert Surveillance Operatives' Clothing Allowance. The Surveillance Agents – more properly the Earwigs – who admittedly had to spend a good number of their working hours in cramped and filthy attics and cellars or huddled in the backs of cover vehicles, put in a claim for an annual allowance to cover the wear and tear on their own clothes. In their opinion this claim was justified by the fact that active field agents – at least down to grade 5C – were granted a yearly sum to cover the estimated cost of one suit, one pair of shoes and three shirts. This extra money was to reimburse them for the expense of replacing clothing lost or damaged in the field, dry-cleaning bills and the repair of items torn on barbed wire or railings, burnt, or – very occasionally – slit by knives or punctured by bullets. This allowance was of course stopped as soon as the agent was removed from active service for whatever reason. Now I felt quite strongly that the Earwigs did not deserve a similar grant, but Black, who had chosen to spearhead their campaign, disagreed with me. Eventually I managed to get my point across by explaining that whereas the Field Agents' Clothing Fund was supported by the special arrangement between MI6 and Lloyds of London, it was doubtful that the insurers would be happy to cover the claims of the Earwigs.

Eventually a compromise was reached whereby any Earwigs who required it could have leather patches sewn on to the elbows of their jackets at the Department's expense.

Neither side was particularly happy with the outcome. Black and I were cool towards one another whenever we met, which is one of the reasons his demands for the cover-tracks meeting and his cable from Beirut had puzzled me. Now I was beginning to get the picture.

'Let me get this straight,' I said, moving away from the uncomfortable seat by the steps to the bunk opposite Gray, 'Philby was the Third Man who tipped off Maclean, Blunt the Fourth Man who helped arrange the defection, and Black was the Fifth Man who blocked Burgess' return.'

'Right except for one small point,' replied Gray. 'Philby was not the Third Man.' Gray settled himself more comfortably and the boat creaked at its moorings. 'Oh he was working for Moscow all right, but he had nothing to do with the defection.'

'But if it wasn't Philby, who did warn Maclean?'

'Shall we say . . . the Sixth Man.'

'Black's handler?'

'The same.'

'Surprise me,' I said, smiling levelly into Raymond Gray's eyes.

'Bill Elsdon.'

My heart seemed to flip over and my mouth dropped open. I believe I felt my flesh creep.

'Surprised?' asked Gray, but I was unable to reply. I

took a shaky sip from the glass and almost choked as the fiery liquid scorched my throat. 'Oh yes,' Gray went on relentlessly, 'Bill Elsdon was mixed up with them all at Cambridge, but unlike the rest of them he didn't keep up social contact with the group. Ploughed his own furrow. He took a big risk when he alerted Maclean in 1951. He knew the Ferrets would be looking for a Third Man and the pressure would be on until they found one. In 1962 he found one for them. Philby's cover had been blown by George Blake and he was now known to have been a KGB agent for years. Elsdon got to him. God knows how he did it, but he persuaded Philby – quite happily it seems – to carry the can. Philby confessed to being the Third Man – even gave a detailed account in the autobiography Elsdon helped him write – and defected to Moscow. Elsdon was in the clear.'

'But then he retired,' I said. 'Why?'

'He was tired. He couldn't afford to break his contacts while the Ferrets and Corkscrews were digging, but once they had their Third Man, he could relax. The last thing he wanted was to be forced to defect. Like Blunt, old Bill Elsdon liked his bit of gracious living. He had no desire to end his days in some pokey little apartment in Moscow, riding round on a bicycle, and queuing for meat in GUM.'

'Where is he now?'

'Last I heard he was running a massage establishment in Bangkok.'

I nodded. Elsdon had been my hero. I took some comfort in the notion that he now may be seeking a kind of redemption in devoting his last years to medical service among the underdeveloped. Traitor though he was, I secretly wished him well in his relief work.

'Of course,' said Gray, 'Elsdon couldn't have done it all on his own. He had his creatures.'

'Oh God,' I murmured, the sheer scale of betrayal only now beginning to strike me.

'The one that fascinates me, Geoff, is the one we might

call the Seventh Man.' I could feel my concentration starting to slip. It was all too much. 'Elsdon's right-hand man, you might say his catspaw. The one who arranged the matter of Maclean's passport, for example, although his greatest service was in pulling the chestnuts out of Elsdon's file and dropping them into Philby's.'

Had a great wave lifted *Water Goblin* and dropped it with a sickening lurch or was it only my mind that had reeled?

'Agent Icarus was Bill Elsdon,' explained Gray as if to a tiny child.

'But I . . . I . . .'

'Poor old Geoff, didn't you know? You are the Seventh Man.'

Sixteen

Gray had refilled my glass and helped sponge the spilled whisky from my trousers. It was a long time before I could speak. Gray sat staring into his glass, and for once he seemed almost embarrassed.

'Whose side are you on?' I asked eventually in what came out as a shaky little voice.

'I'm with the HCKC.'

'Oh are you? What's that?'

'Hungarians. So we hold no great brief for the Russians. Nor do Spiers and his lot, the Chilean Secret Service. Or Lawson. Portuguese.'

'Stop it. Why are you telling me this?'

'Well I hope, Geoffrey old sport, you realize that there is no question of you spilling the beans to Whitehall. Very messy business that would be. You wouldn't come out of it at all well. In fact you wouldn't come out of it at all.'

In spite of the whisky, my mouth was dry. 'You wouldn't tell would you?'

'No.'

'I suppose you just want me to keep quiet about the whole thing? Lie low?'

Gray poured out the remains of the bottle and took a sip. 'Well, that would have been the ideal solution,' he said, slowly turning the tumbler and watching the ripples of whisky crawling up the sides of the glass, 'but that particular line of action has been blocked by a pre-emptive strike.'

'What?'

'Agnes.'

I was already bewildered, but I couldn't follow this at all.

'Not a good idea of yours, Geoff. Dodgy move. After you started fossicking around, pestering her, Agnes started putting two and two together.'

For a while there was silence. An owl shrieked, or a dog-fox or something.

'She's very old,' I said.

'Sharp as an eagle,' said Gray, draining the glass.

'Is Agnes one of yours?'

'Only wish she was, my old love. No, I'm afraid Agnes is one of the staunch few loyal only to HMG.'

'And now she knows everything?'

'Only about you. Worked it out all by her own self. Now I hear she's threatening to blow your cover. No question of lying low if she does that.'

'How do you know this?'

'Elsie.'

I shook my head. Was there no end to these depths of treachery?

Gray pushed himself forward and sat with his elbows on his knees. 'If Agnes goes to Whitehall,' he said, 'a lot of us are going to have to pull in our horns. Sweat it out for a bit. But you will have been named. You, Geoff my old darling, will be thrown to the wolves.'

I felt sick. I stumbled up the steps to stand on the small deck in the biting wind. The night had grown colder and I shrugged the overcoat tighter around me for warmth but it made little difference. Gray joined me.

'What I'm saying is that your contract would have to be terminated with extreme prejudice,' said Gray softly behind me.

I stared bleakly into the night. No retirement pay? No pension? What would I tell Helen?

'Like Dobbs,' he said.

'Dobbs went because he was sick. Then he died.'

'Yes. It took them a long time but they got him in the end. I'm afraid you didn't do a very good job there, Geoffrey.'

'What are you talking about? I had nothing to do with Dobbs. In fact, Burgess once warned me about him. Told me to keep an eye on him.'

'He wanted you to look after him. Protect him. Dobbs was Burgess' contact in the Department. Dobbs knew Elsdon wanted the suitcase destroyed. When he had his one and only chance, Dobbs got it out of their hands and sent it to the raffle. He was aiming to collect it from Mrs Taylor at a later date, then go over and spring Burgess according to the plan he knew he would find in the phone book. Of course, he was never well enough to do it, but he remained a threat. They wanted to kill him straight away. However the assassin, though enthusiastic, was unfortunately inexperienced.'

I wanted to leave then. To run away. I couldn't. Blinking away the tears that the wind had stung from my eyes, I gazed at the scrubby thicket of low trees and bushes ahead of me. At the corner of my vision a little vertical white line moved rhythmically from side to side, ticking left and right, relentless as the Chinese water torture. The drip, drip, drip of Gray's words wearing away my mind.

'Who killed Dobbs?' I asked. Did I really want to know?

'Carol Moon. She was one of Elsdon's creatures. So was that fat boy Armitage down at the passport office. He and Carol had a bit of a fling at one time, I believe. She went cool after a while, though, so nothing came of it. Anyway, Armitage died soon after of Blackwater Fever.'

'Carol,' I whispered.

'Yes, she made contact with you at one time didn't she? That was before Elsdon was sure of you. He put her on to you just in case.'

The little white line was clearer in my eye. Brighter. Tick, tick, tick.

'Is there any more?'

'No more.'

The white line looked real. Something tangible. Reassuring? Threatening?

'What shall I do?'

'You'll have to go over, Geoffrey. To the other side. I'm sorry.'

'Yes. I see that.'

I was numb.

Tick, tick, tick.

Clouds drew back from the moon. The white line was quite plain now. It was a stick.

'What the hell's that?' whispered Gray, following my gaze.

Agnes burst out of the undergrowth some fifteen yards before us. In her left hand she held the white stick, in her right a monstrous revolver.

'Alsop!' she shouted against the keening wind, 'where are you, you bastard?'

'I can't take any more of this,' I said, closing my eyes.

'Be quiet,' hissed Gray, 'she'll know where you are by the sound of your voice.'

The gun went off with a tremendous blast. Warm droplets pattered against my cheek and Gray screamed as he hurtled down the steps into the cabin.

Agnes cackled softly as she got back to her feet. I could hear Gray stumbling about inside the boat.

'Jesus Christ,' he yelled, 'she's shot my bloody ear off.'

Agnes swung round. The revolver boomed again, twice. Spray and splinters flew in the air. Gray howled and shot out of the hatchway past me to land on all fours on the muddy bank. Ears still ringing from the concussions, I could hear the sound of water trickling into the boat, the whimpering sound that came from Gray as he pressed himself flat on the ground, the click as Agnes cocked her weapon.

I stood alone now, quite still on the deck of the slowly

listing cruiser. I had not moved. What was the point?

'Alsop,' growled Agnes, 'you vermin, where are you? Where are you?' her voice rising to a screech, 'where are you?'

'Here I am, Agnes,' I said in a clear, calm voice.

Flinging aside her white stick, she grasped the gun in both hands, pointing it straight at me.

'Treason!' she roared, charging towards the boat.

Agnes was on the other side of the canal.

The thunderous splash sent glistening droplets high into the moonlight. Black mud boiled up from the canal bottom and fat bubbles rose to burst thickly on the surface, releasing the stench of rotten vegetation on the night wind. Ripples spread and rocked the sinking boat as the tumult in the water subsided and nothing was left but a bedraggled hank of hair turning gently in the languid current.

Gray let out a sob. A few yards downstream, with a ghastly spluttering, Agnes surfaced, flailing at the water, the moonlight gleaming hideously on her head. As she drifted away I heard splashing and the twitter of Elsie's voice as she plunged into the canal to rescue her poor, brave, righteous companion.

'Go now,' gasped Gray, his cheek and jaw streaked dramatically with blood. 'Go! It's all over, Geoffrey. Get out while you can.'

I felt lonely and tired and sad. Humiliated. The picture came into my mind of an aged warrior standing in defeat, ridiculous in the remnants of his armour, shield split and weapons splintered, the gorgeous banners of his emperor now trampled in the mud. Or a weeping schoolboy in a windswept lane, his cap flung over the hedge by bullies. It wasn't fair.

But it was over now. Agnes would blow the whistle. There would be nothing left. Had there ever been anything there at all? Gray was right. I would have to go. Grasping the handrail of the boat I set foot on the bank. Clouds once again obscured the pure white light of the moon. Around me there was nothing but the cold and hostile darkness as I took the first reluctant step of what was to become that headlong nightmare traverse to the other side.

The End

Epilogue

I arrived safe and sound in the Falkland Islands two days later. With the help of Gray and John Chappell – my field-man on the other side – the dreadful journey passed off without a hitch. Chappell seems to have a greater loyalty to me than to the Department and he has agreed to maintain my cover.

Life here is dull but not unpleasant. I occupy my time by jotting my memoirs and helping out at the store which handles the distribution of stationery and wool to the islanders. The business is comically disorganized in its ordering pattern of envelopes in relation to the required bulk delivery of paper, and there always seems to be a glut of one or the other. I have been persuaded to develop a consistent policy in this field, and suspect that I shall soon be absorbed into the company at managerial level.

Helen could not be told of my flight until after I had left. I dare say the news upset her greatly, but I sent word to her that she must join me here if and when she can get away without making waves. It will take some time for her to get used to this existence, which is plain and simple. For me, however, it is such a joy and a relief to be away from that world of treachery, double-dealing, dishonesty and betrayal.

For the time being, Raymond Gray has promised to take good care of Helen.

Stanley
Falkland Islands
1981